ABOUT MY TABLE
& Other Stories

ABOUT MY TABLE

& *Other Stories*

Nicholas Delbanco

William Morrow and Company, Inc. / New York / 1983

The author gratefully acknowledges the John Simon Guggenheim Memorial Foundation for support during the writing of this book.

The name of the title story comes from W. B. Yeats' "To Ireland in the Coming Times," and the title "Some in Their Body's Force" comes from Shakespeare's Sonnet XCI.

The stories originally appeared in the following publications: "What You Carry" in *The Bennington Review*; "The Consolation of Philosophy" under a different title in *Prime Time*; "The Executor" in *The Iowa Review*; "Traction" in *TriQuarterly*; "Ostinato" in *The Atlantic*; "Marching Through Georgia" in *Crazy Horse*; "Some in Their Body's Force" in *The Atlantic*; "Northiam Hall" in *The Georgia Review*; and "About My Table" in *Antaeus*.

Library of Congress Card Catalog Number: 83-61367

ISBN: 0-688-02157-3

Printed in the United States of America

First Edition

1 2 3 4 5 6 7 8 9 10

BOOK DESIGN BY LINEY LI

FOR ELENA

CONTENTS

WHAT
YOU
CARRY

His daughter takes after his mother, they say; the two would have gotten along. But there are few who can make the connection, and he avoids it. Kenneth Perrera had prized independence when young; he thought of himself as self-made. Yet he had also been family-proud, able to convey—with just the necessary negligence, the offhand remark that established what it seemed to deprecate—his ancient honored name. Sephardim, his ancestors were bankers. A sixteenth-century Venetian merchant had been famous for his charities. "I've been busily compounding thirty thousand ducats," Kenneth would say, "at seven percent per annum for four hundred years. He gave away my patrimony, trying to buy Christian. It didn't work."

The Perreras came from Portugal and went to Italy, then to Germany and several points in South America. They prospered and were persecuted. His own branch of the family had been entrenched in Hamburg till Hitler caught and slaughtered them. His parents fled to London, where Kenneth was born in the Blitz. He was an only child. When Hitler turned on Russia—or so his mother later claimed—she turned to her husband and asked to get pregnant; it seemed like a gamble worth taking. The odds on survival had never been long, but they had improved.

In 1952 they settled in America; he remembered hiding on the day the *Queen Mary* sailed. On the third day of the voyage out, his parents gave him full-length flannel trousers. He threw his shorts overboard. They ordered caviar each night in the cabin, as if it would be unavailable in the New World.

"Why did we come here?" he asked his mother, later.

Her answer was deliberate. "A country where it doesn't matter what country you come from," she said. "Or which religion. Where everybody's equal and a refugee . . ."

Kenneth did well. He attended Harvard College and Columbia Medical School. He became an internist, with a sub-specialty in pulmonary disease. When in the army he worked—as a major, and in exchange for the years of deferred draft status—at Fitzsimons General Hospital. Denver proved a revelation; he had not traveled west of the Hudson before. But he learned to love the mountains, the air so pure in the pinewoods it felt as if he inhaled clarity with the automatic act of breathing. He began to rock-climb and ski. After the first winter, he met a girl from Colorado Springs. She was a lapsed Catholic and not at all concerned with Kenneth's own lapsed Judaism; they were married by a justice of the peace.

Their honeymoon trip was on horseback. "Let's just disappear," Susan said. "Let's just let the horses find the way." They camped together three miles north of Estes Park. She tethered and curried and fed the horses carefully; she told him that she'd spent her adolescence in a stable. She'd bought the whole mystique, she said, she'd been so fixated on that Palomino of hers she never noticed boys.

Susan wore her blond hair long. She was exactly his height. For years thereafter his favorite photo remained the one he took that afternoon: his bride emerging from a sunshot grove of aspens, the horses' heads behind her, tack draped across her shoulder like a scarf. She wore a paisley cowgirl shirt with mother-of-pearl buttons, and her riding boots accentuated the length of her slim legs.

His mother, too, had been photogenic; he had a leather album showing stages of her age. At first she was a German schoolgirl, carrying a purse and hat and satchel, her hair festooned with ribbons and her walking shoes laced tight. The white of the photograph had faded to ocher, and the black to brown. Her eyes were therefore accurate: large, focused on a spot above the photographer's left shoulder. Some years later, dressed in a fur-trimmed floor-length coat and a karakul cap, she posed in front of a painted backdrop of the Matterhorn. She sported sabots. The next was a full-face portrait of a woman in full bloom: a large-brimmed hat slanted softly from her forehead to high cheek. The lips were Clara-Bow-perfect, their expression both imperious and shy. The throat was bare, the blouse scoop-necked. The one eye not in shadow was astonishing: it fixed the photographer with what Kenneth recognized as disapproval. Perhaps the man behind the box, his head swaddled in black fabric, had been insufficiently respectful when urging her to smile.

She demanded such respect. She was polite in a fashion that unnerved his friends. Through all his adolescence and young manhood this was constant: a continual sense that the woman in an armchair, her reading glasses on and a martini in a water glass on the coaster on the rosewood table at her side, her black hair going gray, her ability to beat him at chess less certain, her German accent decreasing, her roses more splen-

did each spring—a sense that his mother was someone to
reckon with and serve. He was, she said, the apple of her eye.
He brought his girlfriends home for her approval and brought
his laundry home till he was twenty-three. She had a massive
coronary six months after his marriage to Susan, and they
flew east.

His father met them at Logan. Kenneth had been wearing
his army uniform. "You'd better take that off," his father said,
"once we get to the hospital."

"All right."

"It does help with traveling," Susan said. "And we thought
she might be proud."

"No." Simon Perrera was courtly. His gray hair had been
barbered, and he wore driving gloves. "She doesn't like to be
reminded. War. It's not what you should think about when
you've had a heart attack."

"How is she today?" Kenneth asked. "I've talked to Blod-
gett. And Wiesenthal. I mean, how is she feeling?"

His father made a left turn, slowing as he always did and
drifting too far to the right. "What did they tell you, the
doctors?"

"Nothing you don't know already," Kenneth said. "It's
serious."

"She'll be grateful you came," Simon said. "I mean it, both
of you. I know how tired you must be." Simon patted Susan's
knee. "She's been so happy, lately, having a daughter-in-law.
Someone to confide in . . ."

"Someone to complain to," Kenneth said. "About the god-
awful men of the house."

His levity was forced, however, and his father did not
laugh. They parked, and Kenneth extracted a tweed coat from
the carryall. Beth Israel was familiar to him, and the business
of dying had come to seem routine. He took Susan's arm in
the hall.

She lay flat, her face to the window. Her breathing was shallow, her pulse weak; he kissed her cheek, then wrist. She greeted him with no surprise, as if his arrival were normal, as if he had come home from school and not from Colorado two thousand miles away. She had been vain about her skin, its youthful resilience; before bed she had coated it with Elizabeth Arden night cream.

Now it felt dry beneath his fingers. More than any other fact—the charts he read, the consultation with Dr. Wiesenthal in the nurses' station—this desiccation taught him her mortality. His father cranked her upright, and Susan fluffed the pillows. "I want a grandchild," she said.

"There's no rush," Simon told her.

"Not for you. For me."

They spoke in German then, as they had done before he came to understand the language; it had been their stratagem for privacy in public. They had argued, always, with a shared unspoken pleasure in the argument, as though marriage meant continual debate. Susan said she'd like a cigarette, and he took her to the waiting room to smoke. "How do you feel?" Kenneth asked.

"This isn't easy for you, is it?"

"No."

"You said she'll recover. On the plane you said the critical time with a coronary was just after it happened." Susan exhaled. Her eyes were slate-gray and her cheekbones pronounced. The smoke that wreathed her billowed in a downdraft. Her lean shape seemed to thicken, as though with child; he shut his eyes and recognized how much he hoped for just that soft addition to their lives. "Are you all right?" she asked.

"Yes. Let's get back." In Belmont, that night, in his bedroom and the single bed, he made such urgent love to her she worried for his father's sake—that Simon, down the hall alone, would hear her cries. He told her not to worry, that his father would snore through an earthquake. When they were finally finished, he went to sleep on the floor.

Susan had a difficult pregnancy; her morning sickness was severe. She had headaches and anxiety dreams; her lower back gave her great pain. Kenneth told her the adjustments were normal, typical, a question of hormones, not fate. She said it didn't matter why she felt so terrible, but it mattered that she did; they drove together to the Garden of the Gods. This was a favorite outing, a day's drive from Denver with a stop-off at Pikes Peak. But she was out of sorts; she shifted position continually and complained about the altitude; she said that four months more of this were more than she could bear. Her family had moved to Honolulu; she wished that she could visit them and lie beneath the palm trees, drinking rum.

When he turned off the car's air-conditioner, the heat became intense. Susan could not walk. The rock formations greeted them, soaring astonishingly up and out, and all she saw were shapes that boring water made. The multicolored sand seemed garish as a postcard, and she'd seen it once too often anyway. What made them think the Gods would plant a garden in such godforsaken country; why wouldn't they have picked the lowlands where it's green? "Your mother's dying," Susan said. "I'm certain. I dreamed it all night."

"We spoke to her two days ago."

"I know."

"She's fine. She was. You're being superstitious."

"Yes."

Their child was an alien presence as yet, a pillow on her stomach tied by flesh-cords that they could not cut. "I know I'm sounding crazy," Susan said. "I don't mean to be like this. I hate it."

"What?"

She waved at the vista around them, the rocks and scrub and light so white it seemed fluorescent, the tourist buses at the Coca-Cola stand. "This being so far from them. Not only your mother. My parents. Everybody. Our baby. . . ."

"I'll call when we get back," he said.

"No. Now."

So it was from a phone booth in the Garden of the Gods that Kenneth learned of the second, fatal heart attack; his mother had collapsed that morning in the kitchen, cleaning up. "She drank too much coffee. I warned her," Simon said. His voice was reedy, static-riddled. "I said it twenty times a day. 'Don't smoke. Don't drink so much coffee.' She was standing there, Kenny, the pot in her hand. She looked so, so"—his father paused—"surprised."

"I'm coming home."

"We'll be all right. I will be. You don't have to come."

"I'm not sure Susan ought to travel. We're out of town is why you couldn't reach me. But I'll be there as soon as I can."

He watched her through the phone-booth door: a leggy figure with her back to him, wasp-waisted still, their child invisible.

"Surprised," Simon repeated. "That's how she looked. Even with the warnings, Kenny, even when you know you're sick you just can't get prepared. You don't believe you're dying but you die. *Furchtbar,*" he said. "It's a terrible business."

"Yes. I'll call the airlines, okay? I'll make a reservation and then call to let you know."

"Perreras," said his father. "There's only the two of us left."

This time he flew from Denver alone and rented a car on arrival. It was August 25. He spent the trip attempting to marshal statistics on the populace of Leadville, and the influence of altitude on blood volume and pulmonary function. This failed to distract him, however. All through the flight, or drinking gin and tonic at the airport bar, smiling at the Avis girl who told him his smile was contagious, driving, taking two right turns, then a left at the fork by his house—through all the business of travel Kenneth felt himself her boy, behaving. "Punctuality," she used to say, "is the politeness of kings."

She had lived in three countries, she said, and had believed each one would prove her lifelong home. When they take everything away from you, they can't steal what you carry in your head; they can burn the books and confiscate the paintings, or display them in the city museums and not offer compensation—they can strip you of your freedom but not your dignity. She had cousins and uncles who knew the whole of Goethe's *Faust* by heart, or at least all of Part I; they survived Bergen-Belsen and Dachau by reciting Goethe's *Faust*. There had been no copies available, of course, but cousin Arthur Lehrmann had a photographic memory, and his recitation had saved dozens of inmates from death. She had letters assuring her this. For her own part, unhappily, she could remember nothing but the chorus of the spinning song; she recited poor Gretchen's lament:

> *Meine Ruh' ist hin,*
> *mein Herz ist schwer;*
> *ich finde sie nimmer*
> *und nimmermehr.*

Kenneth's German had been poor. He knew the girl was hunting peace, was heavy-hearted since her lover left; he knew that Gretchen's misery was nonetheless in rhyme. He remembered his unkindnesses; he parked. He stood and stretched. When twelve and troubled by their dinner guests' attentions to his mother, having been excluded from their after-dinner coffee and Cognac—though they called it "excused"—Kenneth had offered a toast. "I know a sentence," he said. "Doesn't anyone here want to hear it? I know a German sentence."

"Not now, darling," she said. "Now you can watch TV."

"*Muttie hat dicke Schenkel,*" Kenneth pronounced. "Mommy has fat legs. That's a German sentence, isn't it?"

"It is," she said, her face so dark he could not determine if it flushed with shame or rage. "You can go now. Thank you." He remembered her ten years later, in a hotel in Nan-· tucket. His parents had been on a summer vacation, and he joined them there one weekend after exams. He had taken the long ferry ride, head still stuffed with physiology and jokes about cadavers when the janitor locks up. Gulls cavorted in the wake. He walked to the hotel, jaunty in the bright sea air and feeling like a foreigner; his mother waited for him on the wide veranda. The steps had been sluiced down and scrubbed.

She was sitting in a rattan rocker and, for the only time he can remember, drunk; there were two glasses and an upturned empty bottle of Asti Spumante in an ice bucket. "Well, hello," she said. She waved a hand out at the sea. *"Finalmente."* She tried to rise. Kenneth sat.

"I got tired of waiting," she said. "Your father's somewhere playing golf."

"The ferry was late."

"*Si.* It's sweet."

He lit a pipe. He would give it up that year without reluctance, but the paraphernalia pleased him. He sucked at the pipe stem and puffed.

"I always forget," she said, "just how sweet is Asti Spumante. It's better than Champagne. I mean, if you like sweetness."

"Yes."

"We could have another bottle. I ordered this one for you."

"No, thanks. I'd like a drink, though."

The waiter appeared. Kenneth ordered a Singapore sling. It was his summer for Singapore slings; he had been introduced to them by a girl at the Four Seasons. "Imagine," said his mother. "I can drink Asti Spumante and you can drink Singapore slings. It's as if we were in Italy, for example."

"Have you been swimming?"

"No."

"Is there a tennis court?"

She smiled. "In Portofino, for example, there wouldn't be a golf course. Or they wouldn't let him on, he's such a—what's the expression—'duffer'? What is it you dig up—'divots'? In Genoa, Rapallo, Padua, Siena, Piacenza . . ."

She continued naming cities, ticking them off on her fingers, citing every town in Italy that would not have a golf course. She smiled at her own slurred mispronunciation, saying Fear-*Enzi* for Florence and *Roam*er for Rome. He drank. He put his feet on the porch railing and he also rocked.

"You're looking well," she said. "It looks like you're the one who's having a vacation. But you've lost weight."

"The Cherry Heering in this drink has vitamins," he said. "And so does lemon juice."

"I'm glad I don't have daughters."

"Why?"

"The trouble they would be . . ." She sighed. "The only reason to get married is to have children. I mean it. Don't even *think* about marriage until you want a son."

"I'm not thinking about it."

She smacked her lips, appreciative. "My son who loves ladies," she said. "Thank God that I didn't have girls."

In those next minutes, sitting, watching the sea tilt and rise, waiting for his father and some sense of what to expect, smoking, looking at a family with plastic rafts, a beach umbrella and a Styrofoam container straggle up the stairwell, he came to see his mother the way a stranger might: a drunken, plump old lady at a beach resort. She was flirtatious, nearly; she waved at the waiter and asked for some peanuts or cheese. She giggled; she sawed at the air while she spoke. Her fingers flashed with rings. Kenneth put dark glasses on; sun glinted off a truck. He saw her in the hospital, then dead.

Simon was in the kitchen when Kenneth arrived; he barely looked up from his work. He had his toolkit open and was testing the connections on a toaster oven. These things are firetraps, he said, you could burn the house down just by heating up a roll. It's gotten so bad, Simon said, insurance companies won't pay you for the fire damage if you leave your toaster plugged in; they call it negligence. He himself unplugged the toaster oven every time he used it, and Kenny better learn to do the same. "Your poor mother," Simon said. He indicated the Formica tabletop, the oil and screws and battery, his wrenches wrapped in cloth. "She'd never forgive me. This mess. But I can't work in the basement, with the phone ringing every five minutes. . . ."

He stood. He wiped his hand across his face, then wiped his palms on his pants legs. "I'm glad you managed," Simon said. "I know it wasn't easy."

"How are you, Dad?"

"Don't ask." He turned to the toaster, sheepishly. "This thing is keeping me busy. It does do that."

Kenneth put his kit bag on the pantry steps. The house was airless, and its smells familiar.

"The funeral's tomorrow morning," Simon said. "No formal service, no flowers. Just us." He latched the toaster-oven door, then pushed to release it. "And Susan—how's she feeling?"

"Unhappy," Kenneth said. "I mean, about not being here. We so much wanted Mom to know her grandchild."

"Grandchildren she hoped for," said Simon. "But she knew this was coming—your baby."

"Elizabeth. We'll call her that. We agreed last night to name her after Mom. If she's a girl. . . ."

They sat together for some time, in companionable silence. There was something soothing, always, in his father's painstaking formality. The phone rang but Simon ignored it. "She'll be a girl," he said. "Elizabeth Perrera. And may she make you proud."

Elizabeth did make him proud, in the years to come. She was precocious, an early talker; she walked on her first birthday and memorized whole books by two. She recited what the pictures said, then turned the pages earnestly, so that strangers were persuaded she could read. Her eyes were light blue, flecked with brown; her hair had Susan's texture. They called her Liz, then Lizzie, then Elizabeth; she had been born by Cesarean section, and he stayed out of the room.

He would have been welcome, of course; the doctor invited him in. But Kenneth had asked Susan how she felt about his presence there, and she said she'd rather he waited outside. She hated to think of herself under anesthesia, a slab of meat just waiting to be butchered, and she didn't want her husband to think of her like that. "I don't," Kenneth told her. "I wouldn't. That's not what it looks like at all."

"Still," she said. "You're a doctor. You've been through this before."

"Not with my own wife. Not my baby."

"That's the point."

He offered once more anyhow to be there at her side; she turned her face from him, panting, taking shallow breaths. When the contraction ended, Susan turned to him again; he dabbed at her white face with a wet cloth. "Everything's fine," he assured her. "You're terrific."

"A heroine." She took his hand. He had had enough of hospitals, he told himself, of knowing what the risks might be and what the procedure entailed.

"Just don't hold your breath," he said. "Remember your breathing."

"Yes, sir."

"Yes, Doctor."

"Yes, darling," she said. Her smile was a rictus, however; he had had enough of women in his family in pain. They wheeled her away. He prepared himself in any case, putting on a gown and cap and scrubbing at his hands and wrists and forearms till they shone. He used pumice stone and a nail brush; he repeated this procedure several times. A resident recognized him. They discussed the Broncos' season, then the price of town houses in Aurora; the resident liked ponds. Where he came from, he said, there was so much water in the hills you could rent a dozer for a day and make yourself a swimming hole; a weekend's work and you could dig a lake. "Where do *you* come from?" the resident asked.

"I was born in England," Kenneth said. "If that's what you're asking." He inspected his fingers, and then he turned back to the sink.

Elizabeth at four years old is complicated, inward; she will not go to other children's houses and spends much time alone. She has two pet cats and goldfish and a collection of dolls; she tells them lengthy stories but does not want him to listen. Once he overhears her telling the goldfish that sharks are a problem, and that the cats will cremate them, which is the final game. He asks her if she knows what "cremate" means, and she says of course but will not tell him; it is a secret, she says. She colors things for hours but will not draw freehand; she is meticulous and expert at filling in the blanks. Her favorite books illustrate ballet, and she colors every ribbon of the costumes for *Swan Lake*. "It's anal," Susan says. "It's so tight I can't stand to watch it. One button out of place and she wants to start all over."

Elizabeth likes magazines also; she leafs through them intently. This afternoon she finds a photograph of Henry the Navigator of Portugal. There is a brief biography attached. She points to it. "Daddy, this is God."

"What?"

"This is what God looks like. This is His picture."

It is Sunday afternoon; he has been watching football. There are leaves to rake and bills to pay and phone calls to return, but it is his partner's turn to be on call this weekend; Kenneth feels at ease. He takes the glossy journal. "It's a statue, darling. It's not God."

"It's what He looks like."

"Have you seen other pictures?"

She nods.

"What do you know about Him? God, I mean."

"He's the most important person," Elizabeth says. "Because when you're sick He makes you all better, and when you're dead He fixes you."

Henry the Navigator of Portugal is stern-visaged. He rises from the pedestal as if balanced on a bowsprit, his cape wind-tossed, his arm outflung. Sea-spray from the harbor soaks his beard. Kenneth cannot determine, however, if the statue is of bronze or stone. "I'm not sure I believe in God."

"I do. I pray to Him."

She finishes her apple juice and repositions her Peter Rabbit cup. It has its own saucer and soup bowl and plate. "Who taught you how to pray?" he asks.

"Oh, everybody. Marian."

"And what do you pray for?"

"Peace on earth. Goodwill to men."

He drops the subject, and she asks what time it is. He tells her, and she asks, politely, if he's finished watching football could she watch Disney's *Wonderful World*? "It's not on yet," he says, and she says, "Yes, it is." He turns on the set to disprove her, and Disney's *Wonderful World* is indeed in progress; she says, "I told you so." He pours himself a drink. When

Susan returns from her afternoon ride, she sits on the couch
while he pulls off her boots. The second one works free with a
queer popping sound. "What's the matter?" Susan asks.
He indicates Elizabeth. She is watching alligators, rapt.
The living room is large, high-ceilinged; he need not fear she'll
hear him, but he drops his voice. "Religion."
"What?"
"She's convinced of it. A convert. She's certain there's a
God."
"And Santa Claus too," Susan says. "It doesn't matter."
"Yes, it does. It does to me."
She stands. She pokes at the fire he's built. "Since when?"
A section of cardboard flares, fades.
"Since fifteen minutes ago. Since I learned she's on her
knees at night. Who's Marian?"
"A friend of hers from play group. Why?"
"I'm Jewish," Kenneth says. "My family was exterminated,
remember? This little house painter called Adolf sprayed
roach powder all over the ghetto. I want her to know where
she comes from. I don't want her forgetting that."
Susan wears a turtleneck. She lights a cigarette. "You
haven't done much to remind her."
"All right. But there's a difference."
"Why?"
He will not be deflected. "No daughter of mine is going to
worship Henry the Navigator of Portugal."
She points to Elizabeth, restive now. "Let's discuss it later.
All right?"
"All right."

But, later, things are not all right, are disturbing to him
still. They eat dinner by the fireplace; it is November 18. He
consults his calendar; it displays a picture of the Grand Canyon
at sunset. He thinks perhaps November 18 might be his par-

ents' wedding anniversary but has made no record of the date; he dials his father just in case, but Simon does not answer. It is neither his mother's birthday nor the date of her death, and his failure to identify the meaning of November 18 becomes significant. He thinks of the Battle of Britain, or D-Day, or Election Day, but none of these apply. It is as if he, Kenneth, has lost all sense of ceremony and how the past pertains; he empties the bottle of wine.

"Relax," says Susan. "You're overtired."

"Yes."

"We could go to bed," she says.

He looks at the framed portrait of his mother on the mantelpiece. Simon took it years before. This photo is in color, one of the few he possesses; it shows Elizabeth outside. His mother is wearing a windbreaker, smiling at the sun. The sky is of a bright whiteness, and she wears dark glasses. There is what might be a boat in the background, or a structure that evokes one; water blends with the horizon so that he is not certain if she stands by an inlet, a river or the sea. There is a brown shingled wall to the left.

It is her smile he examines, however, the mouth both expansive and pinched. She is smiling at Simon—from the pleasure of the occasion, perhaps, or the beauty of place, or because of something someone said. It would not have been Simon, however; this is a smile of assent at something more amusing than a request that she smile. Kenneth grows certain, suddenly, that there was a third party present—someone at the edge of things, beyond the lens or range of his remembrance, some business associate of Simon's with a camera, or someone passing through who made his mother laugh. A gull preens on a railing by the wall.

Then Susan yawns and says, "I'm going upstairs, anyhow." He will have to leave for work at seven, she reminds him, he ought to get some rest; the weekend has passed like a day. He arranges the fire and fastens the grate. He lifts Elizabeth from the couch where she prefers to fall asleep. Holding her yellow blanket, she puts her arms around his neck; her breath is hot. He will take her to visit his father on their next vacation, he promises himself; he will invite Simon west. Her legs feel thick where they grapple his waist. "I love you," Kenneth says. "I'm sorry. I so much wanted you to meet."

THE
CONSOLATION
OF
PHILOSOPHY

When he heard his first lover was getting divorced, Robert Lewin panicked. He had not seen her in ten years; they had not been together for fifteen. They had few friends in common; her world was not his world. She was an actress of sufficient fame for her private life to seem public; she smiled at him from newsstands or in the supermarket checkout display. He read about her husband's drinking problem, her near-fatal car crash in Topanga Canyon and their second son's kidney malfunction. The photographs in gossip magazines had captions like "Sally Smiles to Hide the Tears," or "Tragedy Off-stage!"

Robert disapproved. But in a way that was not casual he had loved her all his life; he dreamed that they grew old to-

31

gether, laughing in their sixties at the passion they shared
when eighteen. He was thirty-eight years old, an architect; he,
his wife and daughter lived on the Connecticut and Massachusetts border. Sally would purchase a house near their village.
Knowing that he lived there, she would hire him to remodel
her country retreat. She would want the silo to have two bedrooms and a bathroom, and the barn to be a studio. She would
dam the stream and have him build a sauna and a free-form
swimming pool. All this would be accomplished at long distance, and via intermediaries. She would buy the property
sight unseen, and with all its furniture; Samantha, his wife,
would not know. One bright autumn morning, Sally would fly
in from the Coast to check on her dream's progress. He would
receive her smiling, wearing dark glasses, not old. She would
fold herself into his arms. She would say nothing, since nothing could improve the silence they shared.

At other times he gave her lines. "I never loved another
man," she said. "Not the way that I loved you. It never does
happen again."

"I know."

"It happens differently," she said. "I won't pretend I didn't
love Bill. Our marriage was—well, workable. But no other
man in my life . . ."

"We don't have to discuss it."

"We do. No other man in my life was ever quite as—what
shall I call it, *protective* as you were. Considerate. You *did* take
me under your wing."

Her diction had grown formal. "Is this a performance?"
he asked.

"No. You took care of me. You helped with my homework, remember?"

At this point inventiveness stopped. Robert pictured them
in bed but using their twenty-year-previous bodies; he had not
seen her in the flesh to judge how flesh had changed. His own
had thickened, some; his hair had thinned. Her consorts were

the beautiful people, and he would not fit. His clothes were
out of date. He passed for fashionable in the Berkshires, still,
but felt less and less at ease in cities or with the gaudy young.
He designed doctors' offices and banks. His clients all dis-
trusted what they called the avant-garde. They wanted renova-
tion work and, where possible, restoration. They wanted
contemporary styling with a Colonial theme.

He worked alone. He had a large, illuminated globe on a
teak stand by his desk. When drinking coffee, or in the intervals when concentration failed, his habit was to spin the globe
and shut his eyes and stop its spinning with his finger. There,
where the rotation ceased, he would embark on a new life. He
landed in Afghanistan and northern Italy and the Atlantic
Ocean and near Singapore. With disconcerting frequency, he
landed on the Yucatán peninsula; once he pinpointed Mérida
four times in a row.

The phone rang. "Are you coming home for lunch?" Samantha asked.

"I wasn't planning to."

"All right."

"Has something happened?"

"No. It's just I've got some errands, and you said you
might come home this morning. And I wanted to be here if
you did."

"If you're coming into town," he offered, "we could
meet."

"No, darling, really. I've got forty things to do and might
as well start doing them."

"I'll work right through," said Robert. "And I'll be home
by five. Five-thirty at the latest."

"See you then."

Something in her manner troubled him, as if she called to
know his plans rather than meet him for lunch. He lifted the
receiver in order to return the call, to find her at the house and

tell her he was coming home; his plans had changed. It was eleven o'clock. He did not dial. The prospect of a day without appointments was satisfying, nearly; he shut his eyes and spun and landed in Zagreb.

As the years passed, his years with Sally grew abstract; they both had been beginners, he would say. He forgot the reasons why they grew apart, the bitterness and boredom, and remembered only love. His memory was made up of amorous scenes. He remembered singing with her on a moonlit night in Tanglewood, standing by their blanket in the intermission, drinking rum from his initialed flask and harmonizing on the chorus of "Old Devil Moon." It was 1963; they both played the guitar. Their parents approved. She told him her last boyfriend drove a Thunderbird and wanted to be an astronaut; he probably would be, she said, he understood machines and thought the human body was just another machine. He didn't understand the finer things, spiritual things; by comparison with her last boyfriend—by comparison with everybody—Robert was a prince. Each night when he left her she whispered, "'Goodnight, sweet prince.'" He said, "'And flights of angels sing thee to thy rest.'" She said, "Drive carefully," and he walked backward to the car so as not to lose the imprint of her face. She blinked the house lights three times in farewell; he flashed his car lights also and, for her sake, did drive carefully.

Sally wore her dark hair long. She had a Roman nose and large brown eyes. He called her "almond-eyes" and "beauty" and "love." They took each other's virginity. He remembered how she came to him in her parents' house in Weston, wearing a white negligee and carrying a towel. They spent their college weekends together; he attended Amherst and she, Smith. They embraced in pine lots and in barns and on the rear seat of his Impala and, later, in hotels. They intended to marry as soon as he got his degree. A hollowed-out tree trunk, he said, with a view of the sky would be plenty; it doesn't matter what we do so long as we do it together.

While Robert studied architecture, she applied to and was accepted by the Yale Drama School. They shared an apartment in New Haven, but her schedule and his schedule did not coincide. She performed when he came home from class, and he could not rouse her in the mornings. She dressed in black. They struggled with fidelity; she said she was attracted to Mercutio in her scene-study class. He did not confess to it but slept with a girl in Design; their afternoon encounters increased his passion for Sally at night. When she discovered his affair, she broke their stoneware plates and slammed the cutting board so hard against the counter that it broke.

He could remember how he watched her in rehearsal and saw a gifted stranger. Even then she had the quality of apartness, that silent holding-back the critics came to praise. Her first reviews were raves. They called it "presence," "power in reserve," and when she went to Hollywood, they said that Broadway lost a rising star. Robert lost control. All that fall he called her nightly, running up a telephone bill he had to borrow to pay. He drank too much and worked too little and flew round trip to Los Angeles just to have a cup of coffee with her at the airport. She was living with another man, she said, and would not take him home.

He completed architecture school and elected to practice in Stockbridge, not Manhattan. At twenty-six he married a girl from Springfield; they bought property southwest of town. He modernized the farmhouse and converted the barns. Samantha played the violin and formed a local string quartet; on their sixth anniversary, Helen, their daughter, was born. He prospered; they spent summers on the Cape.

He could have been an actor, people said; his voice was so mellifluous. He could have been associated with such men as I. M. Pei or Edward Larrabee Barnes. Once a friend had said to him, "Don't sweat the small stuff. I see you with a beggar's cup. Saffron robes. That's the kind of change you ought to contemplate, that's the way to get in touch with universal flux. I *see* it. . . ." Robert failed to, but he had been flattered. He carried with him, always, a sense of alternative possibility; his dreams were of escape.

"What's wrong?" Samantha asked.

"Nothing. Why?"

"You're sure?"

He had been splitting wood. He brought in an armload of logs. "It's cold out there," he said. "It feels like snow."

"Is something bothering you?"

"No."

"Do you want to talk about it?"

"I told you," Robert said. "It's only I'm restless. That's all."

"Would you rather I take her?"

"No."

Helen studied ballet. She was plump and unenthusiastic; he had promised to drive her, that afternoon, to see *The Nutcracker* in Springfield. Helen had wanted to go with a friend. "Why can't we take Jessie?" she asked.

"There aren't any seats left."

"How do you know?"

"It's sold out," he said. "I heard it on the radio."

"Jessie's busy anyhow," Samantha said. "Her grandparents are visiting."

"Would *you* come, Mommy?"

Samantha looked at Robert, and he shook his head. He would have liked nothing better than an afternoon of silence, but he had committed himself. He showered and shaved; the forecast was for flurries, so he took the Jeep. "Be careful," said Samantha.

"Yes."

He called her Sam. They were happily married, he said;

she had the kind of resilience he lacked. She lived in the present, he said; if she had an emotion she showed it. If she was angry she expressed it, and the anger disappeared; when she was happy she sang. Helen slept beside him, her seat belt cinching her coat. Beleaguered by desire, he watched the women in the cars he passed, and in oncoming cars. He was, he told himself, just facing middle age, the loss of prowess and mobility that torments every man. This did not help.

He had last seen Sally at a party in Hyannis Port. They had been eating baked stuffed clams and drinking spritzers; his host was saying that he never ate an uncooked clam these days. There had been a hepatitis scare. "It's not as if," his host admitted, "cooking makes a difference. But I feel safer, understand, as if the odds are better when it's cooked." He offered Robert the tray. "It's a kind of roulette we play with our bellies," he said. "It's the bourgeois way of risking things." He discoursed on the difference between littlenecks and cherrystones and quahogs; they were standing on a lawn that sloped down to the shore. "Littlenecks grow up to be cherrystones," said his host. "You understand that, I suppose. And cherrystones to quahogs; it's just a question of when you harvest them. As Marx observes, a sufficient change in quantity means a qualitative change." He lit a pipe. "I always ask myself at what point such change is enforced."

"Enforced?"

"Yes. Decided on. Agreed on, if you'd prefer. When does someone somewhere say, 'Enough. Thou shalt be no more Mr. Littleneck. I dub thee Cherrystone'?" His host laughed and flourished the pipe. "The trial by fire. Sir Clam."

Sally approached. She was wearing white. He felt his stomach tighten and release. "Ah," said his host. "The guest of nonor. How *are* you, my darling? Do you know each other? This is Robert . . ."

"Lewin," Robert said. "Yes. We've met."

She had been as shocked as he, she confessed, but had seen him from the patio. She had been in the area for summer stock, a one-week stint, and was leaving; why is it always like this, she asked, why do we have to go just when we want to remain? He was looking wonderful; his beard made him look like a badger. Was his marriage working out; was his wife at the party?

They made their way to the beach. A rowboat and a Sunfish were pulled up past the tide line, and she settled in the rowboat. He also sat, facing her, facing the house.

"I miss you," Sally said.

"Yes."

"It doesn't change, does it?"

"Not really. No."

"This is horrible," she said. "I wish you wouldn't look like that. I wish I'd come here by myself."

"Who's with you?"

"Everybody. I hide it better, that's all. You should have seen your face—oh, Robert, when that man said, 'Do you know each other?' How *are* you, anyway?"

He scanned the lawn, then patio, then porch.

"All right."

"You mean it?"

He nodded.

"We've wrecked each other's lives, you know."

"No."

"Yes."

"That's overstating it."

With one of those reversals that had made her, always, his equal adversary, Sally said, "Of course. I know I'm overstating it. I'm being theatrical, darling. That's what I do best."

"Other things also," he said.

"But I'm not lying. You lied. You said you were all right."

She shifted weight in the boat. In a movement he could

picture clearly, ten years thereafter, she stripped off her white tights. It was a practiced motion, neither suggestive nor coy; she crossed her long, bare legs. She leaned back on her seat. He asked himself—and would, repeatedly—if she were proposing sex or getting ready to walk on the sand. Her clothing was intact, her sandals and her tights placed neatly by her side. He looked away. Samantha appeared on the porch. Men stood with her, gesticulating. He could hear her laughter. "I hate this," Robert said. He rose; the rowboat rocked. He put one foot over the gunwale. "I want what's best for you," he lied. "And that was never me."

"I'll stay here, thanks," she said. "Goodnight."

"How did it go?" Samantha asked, when he and Helen returned. He hung up his coat. He kicked off his boots. "Terrific," Robert said. "Twenty dollars so she gets to see the bottom of the chair. The part you look at from the floor."

"I closed my eyes, Mommy," she said.

"But what about the Christmas tree? The celebration?"

"I liked *that* part," said Helen.

"And the dance of the Sugar Plum Fairy?"

"He was horrible," she said. "He had big teeth and this enormous tail and his sword was all bloody. He looked like a *rat.*"

"The Nutcracker kills him," Robert said. "You should have watched that part."

"I *told* you," she said, stamping. She turned from him.

"Well, maybe next year," offered Samantha. "Maybe this year was too early for you."

"Let's have a drink," Robert said. "Two vodka Martinis and one hot chocolate for our famous ballerina here."

"All right."

"You do the hot chocolate," he said. "And I'll do the vodka."

They entered the kitchen. Light from the kitchen fireplace played off the copper pots. "Next year," Helen asserted, "I'll be the Sugar Plum Fairy. I will be. You'll see."

Outside, the first snow continued. He had spotlights in the tamarack and maple trees; he turned them on. The garden appeared to leap forward and the kitchen's cage recede. He watched with genuine attention while the fall increased. The grass above the septic tank retained a warmth that melted snow, making a rectangle of bare land on the lawn; it looked like a lap rug thrown over a sheet.

"I don't know what you want from me," Samantha said. "It feels like it's never enough. No matter how much I give, it feels like there's always this one thing left over—this way that we fail you."

"What is it now?" Robert asked.

"She's scared of the Mouse King." Helen was drinking her cocoa in the television room. "So you make it seem *my* fault . . ."

"It isn't your fault."

"I'm not saying that. I'm saying you *think* so; I'm saying you've blamed me all day. As if no child of yours could ever hide under a chair." Samantha exhaled. "As if her sensitivity is something we should apologize for—as if there's something, oh, shameful in a child who has feelings."

"It isn't shameful," he said. He set himself to placate her; he poured another drink. "Control yourself" had been his mother's injunction. Whenever he was greedy, loud or frightened, she would say, "Control yourself. A gentleman has self-control. He doesn't make a fuss about the things he doesn't understand. And if he understands them, there's no need to fuss."

"I love you," Sally said again. She would have purchased Sevenoaks Farm; they would be forty-five. "These barns, that view of the mountains."

"And I love you," he said.

"What have you been up to, baby?" She lit a cigarette. She offered him one; he declined.

"I didn't know you smoked," he said.

"Only when I'm happy. This house makes me happy. And how's your family?"

"They're good," he said. "We live a quiet life."

"You have a daughter, don't you?"

"Helen. Yes."

Sally examined the bay window. "Will you move in with me?" she asked.

"Right now?"

"No. Tomorrow," she said.

His most recent client had been a family therapy center. They had wanted picture windows in the waiting rooms. This had violated Robert's sense of decorum. He said so; they disagreed. There was a village graveyard in the adjoining lot, and he situated the pentagonal structure so the picture windows overlooked the graveyard. "It's tempting," Robert said.

"Be tempted."

"You're serious?"

"Yes. Never more so."

"We've got twenty years," he said. "With luck. Twenty good years, anyhow."

"I'm ready to quit," Sally said. She was emphatic. "I've done enough acting."

"You'll miss it."

"No way. Not for a minute."

He knew enough to know this was not likely. "It's a hard habit to kick," Robert said. "I'm sure it must be difficult. All that applause."

"Those flowers," she would tease him. "Those parties at Sardi's, those feet in Grauman's Theater. Baby, it's nothing like that. It's sons of bitches, ego trips and cameos from here on in."

"You're sure?"

"I'm sure. I've never been more certain in my life."

They would sit in peaceable silence; there were no telephones. They would not bicker as they'd bickered when young; they understood the value of a gentle reticence. The sunset would be doubled by the clear reflecting mirror in the pond and, beneath it, the pool. He dreamed of this in winter while he sluiced down his own pond and scraped it for skating; he dreamed of it that early spring while the ice cracked and thawed. He filled the pool in May. Brian Dennis, after his annual checkup and the lab results, pronounced Robert fit. He redesigned the railroad station, making it a restaurant. Samantha started to jog. She was a natural athlete and soon attained four miles a day. She looked radiant; he wondered what she pictured as she ran.

Their village had a harpsichord maker. He had a shop in West Street, with a sign saying "Master Craftsman" in the window and a harpsichord-in-progress on display. There were marble steps and lintels in the shop, and ornamental hand-carved treble clefs on the door. Samantha knew him, apparently; she mentioned him in passing as a person Robert might enjoy, an adequate instrument maker. He sometimes joined their string quartet to add a piano part. The shop had an apartment on the second floor. Robert, walking to the bank or on his way from lunch or driving home from work, would slow down at the door. He was prepared to ask the price of harpsichords and, perhaps, to commission a lute. The door was never open. There were signs of life, however—fresh piles of sawdust at the workbench, or coffee mugs, or a wastepaper basket filled with what he recognized as that week's Sunday *Times.*

The upstairs apartment, too, seemed untenanted. One day Robert noticed its windows were open, and a woman with her back to him was brushing her brown hair. He stopped. He stood on the opposite side of the street, staring up. There were white lace curtains that obscured his view. He half crouched by a pickup truck; he put his feet on the bumper, one after the other, and pretended to adjust the laces of his boots. He felt exposed, aroused, but could not leave. Her body was supple. She wore a white brassiere that emphasized the pallor of her back. The light was on. She brushed her hair with metronomic regularity, stopping to shift angles every twenty strokes. She was looking at a mirror; he could not see her face. He wondered, was there someone in the room? Her attitude suggested readiness, a knowledge that she might be watched, a sense of self-display. She was familiar, somehow, yet he thought he did not know her: the mistress of the man who made the harpsichords. Her arms were lean. Robert shook his head to clear it, and in that unfocused instant the woman in the window disappeared. Yet he thought he heard her voice. He waited for some minutes, then continued home. Samantha was not there.

He turned thirty-nine in March, and they invited friends for dinner. There were jokes about Jack Benny and the wheelchair he would get next year. "If you think *this* one was bad," said Brian Dennis, "wait till you're forty." Richard Beale had been studying Baba Ram Dass. "'Doing your own being,'" he said. "That's what it's all about, really. Just being here in the here and now. Your health, amigo," he said. "May you be here with joy."

Samantha served poached salmon, and then a rack of lamb. This repeated the menu they shared on their first night as man and wife; Robert was touched. "It's better now," he told her. "You're a better cook than those restaurant chefs."

"You're paying more attention to your food these days."

"All right. I meant it as a compliment."

"I take it that way."

"I'm grateful," he said. "When I said things were better, I didn't mean only the food."

"Happy birthday. Many happy returns of the day."

"'After forty,'" Ellen Dennis said, "'I hold a man's face against him.' Who said that, anyway? I think it was Abraham Lincoln."

"Winston Churchill," Brian said. "It must have been Churchill, not Lincoln."

So they argued over eloquence, and whether Lincoln or Churchill had been the better native speaker, more in touch with the language and times. Jim and Patty Rosenfield had just returned from England, from his sabbatical semester; they contended that the English had a greater native eloquence. "The problem is, however," Jim said, "they all speak so well that you never know who's *saying* something. And who's just making sentences. Even the dumb ones sound smart."

"Another thing," said Patty. "Inflation. You can't imagine how bad it is over there. How expensive everything has gotten. We entertained a little less. Maybe we ate out more often. But at the end of every week we filled two garbage cans."

Richard drank. "What does all this have to do with Lincoln or with Churchill?"

"Waste," she said. "That's what I'm discussing. We throw away more food than all Australia eats."

"I'll drink to that," Robert said. He shut his eyes. The image of Sally assailed him again—some taste or word or smell or sight inciting memory. They were near a sandbar in a saltwater inlet, making love. He lay on his back in the warm shallows, and she sat on top of him. There was a thick fog. Sailors glided in the distance; he propped himself up on his elbows so as not to swallow salt. It was the start of the fall. The cranberries were purple already, and the beach-heather was brown. Gulls watched, incurious. She bounced and settled on him, smiling, her eyes wide. They rented a bungalow called Peony;

it stood in a strip of bungalows named after flowers; their neighbors were Tulip and Rose. The fog felt palpable. He saw himself the sailor now, seeing from the channel how the complicated obscure shape of youth is jointed at the waist; he watched how fleetingly they fused and broke apart. He toasted his guests and his wife.

They kept in touch, but distantly; a friend of friends said, "Sally sends regards." Her telephone number was unlisted; she sent it to him in April and wrote, "Hope to hear from you." By the time he did call, from his office, a recorded voice pronounced, "We're sorry. We cannot complete your call as dialed." He was not sorry, he decided, he would not have known what to say. Panic is the fear engendered by the great god Pan. He comes to the party unannounced and overturns the chairs and spills his drink on the rug. He will attempt his magic trick with the tablecloth. He scratches his beard, paws the floor.

Promising the cutlery and plate and crystal will remain in place, he whisks the white linen away. He is clumsy, however; things crash and tumble all over. The girl at the head of the table gets wine on her jumpsuit. She scrambles to her feet and scampers down the hall. He follows her, apologetic. There are remedies. They huddle together. There are dry cleaners, other parties, prospects of the sea. There is time.

Wind rattled at the pantry door when she opened the door to the mud room. She settled her handbag and two paper bags on the bench.

"You're having an affair," he said.

Samantha took off her gloves. She placed them on the shelf. "Was that a question?"

"No."

"Good." She shrugged out of her coat. "It didn't sound like a question."

"Are you having an affair?"

"In any case"—she selected a hook—"I don't think I'll bother to answer."

"His harpsichord. How quickly can he build one?"

"That depends," she said.

"He's careful?"

"Yes."

"Attentive?"

"Very."

"A master craftsman," Robert said.

"I've been downtown, master. Shopping." She opened the mud-room door again. "In case you're curious."

"Yes."

"Be careful with the eggs," she said. "They're in the bag in the Jeep."

In June the local ballet school offered a performance. It ran for three successive nights, and each was sold out in advance; the children came home from rehearsal with their allocated tickets. Helen was in the school's youngest class, but there were students all the way through high school. The program was immense. Its theme was that of "The Magic Garden," and children were divided, according to age and experience, into several units: there were butterflies and inchworms, bumblebees and bunny rabbits, a group of birds and flowers and scarecrows. The soloists were labeled Spring, Summer, Autumn, Winter; there were twelve such soloists, with four to perform on each night. The owner of the ballet school was, as she put it, *bouleversée;* she made a speech before the performance and said she was just so excitable because of these wonderful wonderful students that *bouleversée* was her only expression; we are enraptured to see you all here.

Helen was a Black-Eyed Susan; she wore a bright green tutu and brown leotard and fitted orange cap. There were twenty other Black-Eyed Susans, and they skipped onstage, then curtsied and circled and whirled. Helen did so by herself. Then they all joined hands and did what looked like the Virginia Reel; fathers filled the aisles and, using flash attachments, photographed their girls. Robert had not brought his camera. He had had a long afternoon. He had come directly from the office to the auditorium; there were problems with the railroad ties he'd used for decorative beams.

During intermission, he could not find Samantha in the sea of women and daughters waiting in the hall. He pushed through swinging doors to what would be backstage; the Rhododendrons and the Owls were doing warm-ups by the barre. There were belly dancers also, waiting for their turn in "The Magic Garden"; they wore veils and diaphanous skirts. Mothers were removing rouge and lipstick from their daughters' upturned faces. Helen said, "Hi, Daddy."

He looked for her.

"Hi. Here we are."

Samantha closed her makeup kit. She stood.

"Well, look at you," said Robert. "You look beautiful."

"Thank you, Daddy." Helen pursed her lips, demure.

"Doesn't she?" Samantha said. "How do you like these sequins?"

"Very much," he said.

"The ponytail?" asked Helen.

"Yes. You'll be a star."

All around him, Robert knew, fathers were thinking the same of their daughters; all around him the girls were transformed. She was, he said, his precious ballerina, his precocious soloist. A belly dancer brushed past. "Do you want to watch the second half?" he asked.

"I'm tired, Daddy."

"You?" he asked Samantha.

"I'll tell the Cartwrights we're leaving. We got a ride down here with them, so we could all go home together."

She was, he told Samantha, wonderful. Helen wore eye-liner and mascara and had not smudged her lipstick or her rouge. Samantha turned and, bending, began to scrub at the upturned face. "Leave it," he said to his ladies. Helen wore her tutu to the car.

THE
EXECUTOR

It had been snowing. This was the season's first storm, and the tamaracks were brown, not bare; oak leaves lay on top of the snow. Edward built a fire, then made himself a drink and settled to read. The letters were a jumble—thrown into a cardboard box that crumbled at the edges. Bits of paper came loose in his fingers, and he inhaled decay.

He had had trouble driving home; the weatherman used phrases like "snow alert" and "traveler's advisory." He had lived in Massachusetts for ten years. Yet every year, at the first snow, Edward felt just such a shrinking fear—as if he had to hibernate but would be unprepared. The certificate of death for Jason Simpson was a photostatic copy, black, reduced. Category 6a of the personal particulars read: "Usual Occupation

(Kind of Work Done During Most of Working Life, Even If Retired.)" The examiner had typed in "Artist." Category 6b read: "Kind of Business or Industry in Which This Work Was Done." This space was blank.

"You remember the Simpsons," his father had said.

"Barely."

"It wasn't *all* that long ago. They died in—let me see— 1966."

"That's long enough," Edward said. "I was just finishing college."

"Yes. But you do remember them."

"A little," he admitted. His father's nostalgia was its own system: the stories he told seemed pointless, self-regarding. Edward (home for Thanksgiving, slicing the overlarge turkey, ignoring their questions about the pending separation and where Marcia might be this holiday weekend, telling his cousin, "The truth is we woke up one morning and turned to each other and said the same thing: 'Does it have to be this way? Do we have to go on for the next forty years?'. . .") bent to his plate.

"They loved *you,* apparently. Jason *and* Nadia," his father said. "They wanted you to have this packet. *I'm* the executor."

Edward was preoccupied. He tried to scan the pattern of his father's emphases. His wife had flourished in such celebrations; she liked the bustle and clatter.

"*When* you're thirty-five years old. It's a stipulation," his father finished. "Which you are now. So that's *their* life story, this box."

"All right," he said. "What do I do with it?"

"Take the thing home. Sell it. Burn it. Whatever you want; it's *your* business, Eddy, not mine."

Driving north the next afternoon, as rain turned to sleet then snow, he summoned up the Simpsons' images again.

They had been his father's friends—thin elderly people, the man in a wheelchair, the woman's skin translucent. Even as a child, when the distinction in age mattered little, Edward knew his father's friends were a generation older: family dependents somehow, on the dole. He remembered an apartment cluttered with canvas, vaporizers, and a blown-glass antelope they gave him that he broke. Edward was examining it—pleased beyond caution by the intricate fretwork—and shifting it from hand to hand when the pink creature fell. He remembered the small shattering (a tinkle more than crash, a little set of splinters at his feet) and the horror of having to sweep the thing up. Old Jason Simpson told him not to worry, never mind, but he picked every shard from the rug.

Edward came from Scottish stock. He used Scottish expressions with frequency and made much of his ancestors' "deportment." They were sheep-stealers, he claimed, and had been deported for taking one North country Cheviot too many through one stile too few. "I like to think of Philip," Edward said, "my great-great uncle's great-great-uncle. Caught in the midst of bogs or fens or wherever it is the laird does the catching. With a sheep stuffed up his kilt in imitation of Gammer Gurton's needle. 'What's that you're hiding, Philip?' the laird on horseback asks. He asks this not unkindly, for there's humor in the scene. The sun is westering; we have echoes of the drum and bagpipes, lewd music mostly. 'Nothing, milord,' Philip answers. 'Nothing but what any man who has it has to cover.'

"'A fair thought, nothing,' answers the literate laird. 'To lie between maids' legs.'

"'Milord?' inquires Philip—whose bumpkin learning has not embraced *Hamlet*.

"'Ah, maun ye mock me?' inquires our laird—a collateral

cousin to poor Bobbie Burns. 'There's not a lassie lying ten miles aboot who'd let that beastie baa at her.'

"For indeed the North country Cheviot bleats. In vain my cornered ancestor attempts to call it broken wind; in vain he claims himself full-fleeced around his parts. The laird ups with his kilt and outs with his guilt and away goes the clan to America . . ."

And Edward would tender his glass. He told the story better on his second drink than third. Then he included border dogs and made reference to "wool gathering" in *The Second Shepherd's Play*. On his third drink, also, he would speculate about the tall tale's "thread" and "darn good yarn"; he told the story often and, he was persuaded, well.

Some letters were in envelopes, some torn. His father's generosity was real. There were postcards and letters and offers of help, then the legal structures of support. His father sent them a small monthly check, arranging that ten other patrons do the same. His efforts on their behalf (with museums, with the landlord who had tried to raise the rent, with the City of New York when they required nursing care) were, it seemed to Edward, ceaseless.

Then he discovered his own scrawled thank-yous from twenty years before. If the Simpsons sent him an Indian headdress, he sent them a poem about it; when they congratulated him on his acceptance at Yale, he sent them a self-deprecating cartoon. Edward drew "a bulldog leading meek me by the leash," and, half his life later, feeling the tug of propriety, recognized the truth in his cartoon. When they sent him a book about Joseph and the Nez Percé—the last gift; he'd turned twenty-one—Edward responded politely, saying that he had a waning interest in these matters and they were kind to remind him. Later he had come to realize that the warrior-chief was emblematic to the crippled Simpson: the admirable outlaw in him had been shot.

"Why are you giving me these?"

"They're yours," his father repeated.

"They're valuable."

"I wouldn't know. It's your *business,* Eddy; you're the curator."

He said "curator" as others might say "doctor"; Edward changed the subject. "How are you feeling?"

"All right. I've been to Meyrowitz." His father shrugged. "I'll live."

"What about the holidays? If you'd like to come . . ."

"Eddy, I can't keep this with me any longer. There's only so much I can keep in the closet. You follow? What'll happen to these things? I ask myself; someone should make sense of them. Not me."

His father coughed. It had taken him years to propose that Edward's life was wanting. He had not been reproachful. They rarely met; his father carried independence to the point of indifference, Edward complained.

"That's reciprocity. His way of getting even," Marcia said. "It's how you used to behave."

"With whom?"

"With everybody," Marcia said.

"You flatter me," he said.

Edward spent his life at art: handling and appreciating and assessing and paying the freight. He bought and sold and owned and restored it, always respectful, curatorial—always, he told himself, bored. Why should a man as sane and sweet as Jason Simpson seemed—why should a figure so compounded of decency, ambition and a stubborn sense of making—make no difference finally? There's no madness, Edward thought, like that of the gambler in art; the horseplayer, lottery addict, the lady at the one-armed bandit dawn by dawn in Vegas, all have better odds. Now he handled the receptacle of some long-dead adept's efforts, and he had to read it through.

There were letters from men who went to Pamplona in

the wake of Hemingway and girls who learned to cook with
Alice Toklas. In the thirties the notes were trilingual—spiced
with German phrasing, laced with Italian or French; notes
from England in the forties made no mention of the war.
There were thank-you letters, Christmas cards, apologetic letters for "the length of time we've been apart" and promising to
write more often soon. There were lawyers' letters, bills, re-
ceipts, the leavings of the fifty years that Simpson had spent
scrambling for a toehold and safe perch. His wife received
few letters; he was the family scribe. There was a packet of
his correspondence when her breakdown kept them separate,
or when he worked in California making murals for three
months.

John Marin sent a map to where they spent the summer.
Someone had scrawled in the margin, "Hope you'll find it possible to visit. Dew Drop Inn!" e. e. cummings thanked the
Simpsons for their birthday gift, and Stieglitz, answering a request for assistance, countered with needs of his own. Girls
Edward had never heard of sent back impressions of Paris; a
woman on an ocean liner sent them sketches of the waves. The
language was formal or tub-thumping; the writing meticulous—Marianne Moore's—or barely legible—E. Walsh's.
There was such a sense of energy, of time forever on their
side, of the instant's immortality for all that generation:
Thomas Hart Benton hoped Jason would feel better after his
damned stroke.

Wind forced the cat-door open; Marcia had taken the cats.
When he closed the door again, the latch proved inadequate,
so Edward propped a log against the door. Wind found its
perimeter and blew past the four sides. He imagined the chill
rectangle advancing till it shaped itself, intact, upon the room's
far wall.

He himself had hoped to be an artist, once. He'd bought, as he told Marcia, the great American dream. This consisted of paint-spotted tweeds, an unlit pipe, unruly hair, the wild-eyed glint behind sunglasses that signified a man could *see*. Write in water, paint in sand; scan *The New York Times* each Christmas for some mention of your year's accomplishment, and year by year accept oblivion because Picasso and ten others reap rewards.

But he'd always known himself, he claimed, you had to give him that. Even at twenty he had suspected what his twenties proved: that art was a necessity for others, luxury for him. He painted an acrylic version of "The Rape of the Sabines." He conceived a three-act theater piece about the life of Byron, entitled "Curious George," to be performed in drag. It's what to do when the dishes are done; it's not flourishing in China where they force-feed equality.

So Edward painted as an avocation, not vocation, but quite well. His degree was in art history, and he took a job, when twenty-eight, as assistant to the Curator of Prints and Drawings in a museum in the Berkshires that was privately endowed. His reticence seemed pleasing; his ignorance had been construed as modesty by the dowager who hired him. She owned a Jason Simpson drawing of the Statue of Liberty in rags; it was inscribed to his father, and she recognized the name.

The work was undemanding, and he settled in. Edward organized the files, reorganized the cabinets and had the Flemish collection uniformly framed. He rented a small white clapboard farmhouse on the edge of town and, once assured of permanence, he bought. The last time we changed staff, his secretary said, was after the *Titanic* sank. At a black-tie testimonial dinner in honor of the donor of a set of Goya etchings and a portrait by Franz Hals, he met his future wife. Marcia was the director's niece, up for the fall foliage, she said, just mad about the oaks. When he realized that she said this with the edge of mockery, not meaning "mad about about the oaks" but to establish that she thought the phrase was foolish, and the celebration, and the solemn, owl-eyed scrutiny of "Los Caprichos," Edward asked her to come home with him for a postprandial snort.

"If you mean coke," she said, "no, thanks."

"I didn't mean that," Edward said.

She also noted mockery and, noting this, accepted him; they shared a bottle of Remy Martin.

That night he built a fire, heralding the fall. "I usually don't drink this much," she said.

"Say 'usually' five times," he said. "If you get the last one right you're sober."

"Usually, usually, usually, usually"—she paused for breath and laughed. He watched her red hair glinting in the firelight, the coppery tones and cheekbones that seemed Indian in emphasis, and said, "All right. You've proved it. You're the perfect figure of sobriety."

"Picture of sobriety," she said. "That's what you mean. Not figure."

They kissed. They fell against each other on the hearth like warriors. Her body surprised him—the lean conformation under what he first had noticed, her breasts. "I thought there was more meat on you," he said. She laughed and told him that she always felt too cold up here and therefore wore too many clothes, an extra layer to keep men like him away. "I'm glad it didn't," Edward said, and she raked her fingernails along the inside of his leg.

Three months later, when they married, Edward said he'd found a home at last; Marcia said she knew exactly what he meant. His job was secure; they owned the house and two cars. Saturdays he set up his easel in the garage and painted still lifes there, and a portrait of his bride with coconuts. She en-

couraged him; she said she liked his sense of line, the dark and
cutting range of the palette.

Simpson made rag dolls; he collected kachinas. He had an
eye for horses and did variations on a circus theme. He was a
colorist whose cityscapes and seascapes used the same shade
of blue. "What do you think of this painting?" he asked.

Edward had studied it, shy.

"Don't be embarrassed," said Simpson. "Just tell me what
you see."

"See?" He squinted at the riot of color and shape.

"Don't *read* it. Don't tell me what you want to see. Just
describe what's there."

Nadia nodded, encouraging. She had a plate of sugar
cookies and she gave him two. He chewed one; it tasted of oil.

"I mean *literally,* boy."

"There's a dancer," he said. "There's what looks like a
camel he's leading."

Simpson took a cookie also, and he held it poised. With
his left hand he turned the wheelchair full circle.

"Maybe that's a tower, I can't tell," said Edward. "The
green thing sticking up back there. Maybe a windmill. Or
trees?"

"You're just pretending." Simpson licked his lips. "You've
lost the gift of sight, my boy. It's not your fault. It's how they've
taught you, everything you've learned for all these years."

"It *is* a windmill," Edward said.

"You were closer the last time. 'That green thing sticking
up back there.' That's what you saw."

Nadia patted his arm. "Don't worry," she offered. "We all
forget what we knew. What do you see, for instance, when you
look at Jason?"

"A man about sixty. With white hair. A painter. Your
husband."

"No," Simpson said. "Wrong again. You were right about the white—the rest of it, though, is invention. Accurate invention, as it happens, I grant you. Sixty-seven. But what you *saw* was this green shape you're thinking should be 'sweater'; what you see is orange here, and a blue mass above it, then two brown things that, for the sake of convenience, we'll call pants. You've got to make up the world, boy, see it as you saw it when you only saw the undersides of sinks." He threw out his arms, theatrical. "The day you decided those pipes and that bowl meant 'toilet'—function, not form—that was the day you went blind."

Edward added ice. Suddenly he understood the reason for their gift. The old man must have seen him as a caretaker, curatorial even then. So this bequest had been self-serving also, not selfless or random. Edward knew he'd seemed the logical successor to his father's stewardship—the next supporter, Jason might have said, by right of bourgeois birth. They'd predicted his career. If he hadn't ended up in the back offices of some Berkshire museum, he'd nonetheless have access to the place. Jason might have guessed as much—had been responsible, even, in the course of that first interview for Edward's very hiring and would expect compensatory thanks.

He poured a second scotch. He stretched, switched off the reading lamp. That he should be predictable—who'd lived his professional life in order to encourage and justify just such prediction—irritated him. He drank. He said aloud, testing the phrase, "They've left me holding the box." He thought the substitution amusing, mildly; he bit the rim of his glass.

Then the irritation passed and he stared at the fireplace. It was deserved, after all, and there'd been value in the gift; he could sell the notes by cummings and the map Marin had drawn. He could turn their loss to profit, judiciously, then pay his father back. Edward felt his concentration slacken and re-

lease. Whatever problem he'd been set to solve was slipping
from him cozily. He shifted his weight, stretched again. And in
the succeeding instant he felt rage—shock after shock of it,
jolting. He stood. His adult life held no such anger; he was a
child again, biting the bedspread, kicking at whatever he could
kick. He tore at his nails with his teeth. Out there beyond the
bedroom there was expectation's tyranny: he was nothing
original, nobody, never had been or would be.

Edward threw on a birch log. It came to him—alone, in
his well-appointed house in the foothills, standing by the
fieldstone fireplace, with its oak mantel bearing Tibetan wood-
blocks (four of them, acquired from the Victoria and Albert, of
elephants with maidens on their jewel-encrusted tusks, the
great-limbed heroes dancing)—that he would leave. He
pressed his nose to the living room window and peered out.
The tamaracks were dark.

Marcia would be with her lover now in Roland Park. She'd
acquired children—three from his first marriage—and would,
Edward imagined, be making turkey soup out of their supper's
leavings. Thanksgiving must have been a shock to her. The size
of the turkey, the number of portions of yams and chestnut
puree and bowls of cranberry and rice and gravy and relish,
and cornbread—all this evidence of family might give her
pause. There would be traditions in which she had no part; the
weight of the wineglass felt wrong.

"What you don't understand," she had insisted to Edward,
"is ambition. It's wanting to count in this world."

"No."

"Yes. To make a difference. To be able to say, when you
walk in a room, 'I matter. I'm here. This is me.'"

"That's vanity," said Edward. "Or arithmetic. You're only
talking addition."

"Ambition."

"*Count*," he repeated. "A *difference*. Assertiveness training, that's all."

Then she seemed deflected by his parrying agility, and
they made peace. She wanted a shower, she said. They agreed
that they each had been wrong. She would stand at the counter
he had never seen, wearing the apron he'd bought her (or
maybe something with oysters and lobster on it, since she'd
moved to Maryland, some chef's hat over pastry shells that
spelled: "Welcome to Chesapeake!"), ladling soup. He could
imagine it precisely: the size of the carrots she sliced, the stalks
of celery she'd wash with brisk inattention.

"I'm leaving you," she said that night.

"When?"

"As soon as possible."

"And who are you going to?"

"Edward . . ." she began.

"Notice I didn't ask *where*. Notice I know that it's someone, not somewhere." He focused on her ear. There was a
turquoise pendant he could hook his finger in.

"Harrison."

"In Baltimore?"

"Roland Park," she said. "There's a difference."

"He's the one with all those brats?"

"They're not brats."

"I'm only saying what you said. You called them brats,
remember? Why'd you pick that one?"

She sighed and spread her hands. She said, "You flatter
me. I didn't have that much choice."

Marcia had the gift of prophecy. She saw things when she
shut her eyes. She saw jessamine and wisteria and azalea
blooming in the courtyard or in winter sleet. She could tell,
the night before, what color the baker's wife's apron would be
when she changed it next day. She had never seen an orange

grove, but she knew the way an orange grove in California looked—a certainty not based on but attested by the postcards she'd received. Someone could describe the Isenheimer altarpiece—and Marcia shut her eyes and saw Mathias Grünewald in a frenzy of invention, and she *saw* what he had had to eat and the paint stain on his index finger and the way he chose to rectify his first version of the foot. She had pictured Edward standing in their house.

That was before they met. He was standing in the kitchen; she had recognized the gas stove right away. He was wearing blue work clothes but the sun poured in so brightly from the window by the pantry that she could not see his face. He had been waiting for water to boil; he whistled but she could not hear the tune. That first evening at the banquet—did he remember the watercress soup?—she had seen the menu by the time they reached the door.

Edward had been dubious. He made up explanations or ascribed it to coincidence if she reached to take the phone before it rang. She would press her head and hold it at the instant of a car crash miles away. Four-leaf clovers fairly leaped at her from roadsides and in meadows. He asked her how she found them, and she shrugged and said she never looked, just something about the pattern forced itself on her attention.

Edward heard two village churches where he sat. Their clock towers did not agree. One chimed the hour three minutes earlier than the other, and the half- and quarter-hour chimes were discordant also. That three-minute interval became the stuff of anxiety, an emblem of exactitude that had turned inexact. One of the clocks was correct, but he could not identify which. His own watch halved the interval, so possibly they both were wrong and he should have heard a third chime.

It was ludicrous, he knew, to squander his attention on the clocks. He thought of crepes suzette, of Caravaggio, of every woman he had ever slept with and whether the initials of their names comprised the alphabet. He reached "I" with no trouble, and he had two candidates—Zoe and Zara— for "Z." But he ended up unable to provide a woman who began with "I" or "Q" or "X." He assumed that this was commonplace, that women with those first initials would be, by comparison, rare. Edward took comfort in his memories, their unsurprising result. Then the first clock started in.

Was it possible, he asked himself, that he in this entire kingdom of the one-eyed would prove blind? Everywhere he saw the visible world intensely: a blade of grass sheeted with moisture, a cloud whose billowing edge was strange shapes, a wall that needed paint. Yet those who looked at him saw nothing, a translucency. Marcia saw him as a man to be dismissed.

"Drive carefully," his father had urged him.

"I will. I'm sorry," Edward said. "I've been preoccupied."

His father was an earnest man—tall, stern. He wrote letters to the editor and to his congressman about the shameful way this nation treats the elderly. He himself was fortunate to have both health and a modest retirement income, but everywhere he turned he found people were less fortunate than he. "I'm glad you came," he said. "Thanksgiving is for the family. It's a family *occasion,* and that's right."

"Can I ask you a question?"

"Of course."

"Tell me why you did it."

His father adjusted his glasses, quizzical. They were standing at the door.

"Took care of the Simpsons, I mean."

"*Did* it?"

"Yes."

His father touched the box. "It isn't something to do," he said. "It's a way of being. A way to be."

"'They also serve who only stand and wait,'" said Edward. "Is that what you mean?"

"Not at all."

Nadia had something to tell him, she said, something she ought to explain. Jason got excited by visits, so nervous he should have a rest—she patted Jason on the head and told him she'd take Eddy to the store because Eddy could bring back the bags. Those steps, she said, were getting steeper; she could use the help. Did Jason want to close his eyes while they were at the hardware?; she'd return in a jiffy with linseed oil and light bulbs and toilet paper and, if he behaved himself, some of Gristede's corned beef.

Her excitement was transparent. She clattered down the steps like a schoolgirl, string bag slung from her wrist. She took his arm at the corner, saying, "Guess what, Eddy? I wanted to tell you. It'll be such a surprise." He piloted her across the street; she stared at taxis and the halted, idling cars. "The museum called yesterday," she said. "Mr. Moneybags. He didn't say so, of course, they're far too cautious, curators, but what they were asking—I can tell, I haven't been with Jason all those years for nothing—what they were asking was would we sell those charcoals he did on our visit to Scotland? You remember, don't you, the Glasgow mills at dawn? You remember the pictures, I mean. Those great big blokes—is that what they call them?—all covered with coal dust, their eyes like whitecaps on a positive black *wave* of faces, Eddy, the dogs, the grass that he managed to make look wet so you just knew it was raining . . ."

Nadia paused. What she needed to tell him was not this, she said; she needed to say something else. She had been planning ever since Edward arrived to get him outside on some sort of errand and tell him that Jason was dead. She could smell it in the room. He must have noticed, hadn't he, the stink on the wheelchair when Jason wheeled up? He was dying even if the doctors couldn't see it, and their prescriptions and advice and optimistic machinery were helpless. Nadia blew her nose. She lived with him, was there each day and every moment of each day, she knew how his breathing had changed. What will I do, she asked, how can I go on without him, how will I ever continue?

They walked the aisles. He helped her gather nails and flashbulbs and turpentine and paper towels. At the plumbing fixtures section, Nadia extended her hand. She fingered a display of faucets, smudging the sheen. "My life is his," she said. "His life is me. I can't live without him, I haven't the skill. It's what I told the man who called, the one from the museum: I haven't the skill or desire to live while my Jason is dead."

Therefore he piled the sheets—precisely, using paper clips, then rubber bands for decades. He filled the box again. The folder for the forties bulked the least large. The fire snapped and crackled at him, and he fed it with a pine bough that flared. "It is my wish that I be cremated. Please take care of this matter." Edward knew the indicated gesture was now to feed this fire with the ranked packets before him. The flame was picture-perfect, the length of the log: high, hot. He rearranged the box. He pictured its consumption: first brown, then black, then crepitant, a shapeliness adhering to itself.

For several minutes he conjured the Simpsons. Their death had been a release. He studied the certificate and its grim declension: of natural causes, attested in triplicate. They had lived together fifty years, and he was separated after four. He found a postcard addressed to the hospital in East Islip, where Nadia had been sent in 1932. "Sweetheart," the legend read. "I send you all my love, and hope things improve for us always." There was a watercolor of a man on a horse, doing a handstand with a beach ball on his upraised foot; the sweep of the balancing act carried across to the stamp.

He would not, at any rate, burn the letters. He rose and

took the box—through the kitchen door, then the storm porch and down the stone steps. There was ice on the trees. He wore no coat or gloves and shivered, inhaling. Edward smelled his own fire's downdraft; the sky had cleared. His wife had planted tulips in abundance just before she left him, saying, "Why not, after all, what else would we do with these bulbs?" He'd helped her make a flowerbed beneath the western wall. That ground was open—protected from the blowing snow, and warm enough so that what landed was melting. He placed the carton, carefully, in the center of this wet dark strip. It would weather the winter, then shred.

TRACTION

W hen Alexander was informed his daughter had a dislocated hip, he had no clear image of the operation involved. He had visited his dying mother, friends in pain and wife in childbirth, but disease had always been at a remove. He imagined traction, then the knife. He nodded sagely at the doctor, seriously, his mind a cartoon-riot of shapeless things in plaster, their Ace bandages raveling, legs hiked high. There is always a one-line tag, but Alexander could not read it. The doctor was saying, "Ten days."

"Ten days at the most?"

"For traction, yes. On the average, Mr. Cullinan. We'll have to keep testing and see."

"It could be less?"

"Could be." The doctor sounded dubious. His hair was long, coat white; he was in training for the marathon and had been trained at Massachusetts General. He was an expert, they said, an excellent orthopedic surgeon, the best in this town. Jane was with their elder daughter at ballet; therefore Alexander had brought Gillian alone. She lay in her snowsuit, eyes wide.

"How do you test for it?"

"By X-ray. Ten days is a ballpark figure. We'd hoped the Pavlik harness would have done the trick."

"We'd hoped so too," said Alexander When their baby had been fitted for the harness, six months before and six months old, they'd thought it cruel confinement; now it seemed like freedom by comparison with what would come. Freedom's a comparative, he thought; the sling was of an airy lightness and had not hampered her. She had been learning to crawl.

"You understand," the doctor said. "It's not so early anymore. It's frankly dislocated now. We can't afford to wait."

"I understand that. But a second opinion . . ."

"Of course. You should take her to Boston."

"Yes."

"Take the X-rays with you and let's hope they disagree." The doctor smiled, not meaning it. "I'll set up the admission here for Tuesday."

"Is there any chance the traction will be adequate? I mean, just traction? That you won't have to operate?"

Her X-rays filled the envelope. They were encased in cardboard but felt leaden nonetheless. "No. I'm afraid not. None."

"Thank you, Doctor."

"You're welcome."

"I'm sorry to have taken so much time."

"That's what we're here for."

"It does surprise me," Alexander said again. "We had such faith in the harness."

They stood. They were of the same age and height. Gillian opened her arms, and he hoisted her up from the table. His authority, however, had been relinquished in the waiting room. The doctor took some seeming relish in bringing the lawyer to book. "We've got to make the best of it," he said. "It won't bother the child if it doesn't bother the parents. You'll be surprised at how adaptable they are. She doesn't know what walking's like, remember; she won't miss it. And in any case we've got no choice—we've waited as long as we can."

He drove to Boston the next day, with his three women on the back seat of the Jeep. His wife was drinking heavily. She had periodic bouts with what she called her first lover, Jack Daniel's, though she had had affairs with George Dickel and Jim Beam and Ezra Brooks. She cradled a fifth of Jack Daniel's; their four-year-old, Suzanne, was sleeping in her lap. The Cherokee had poor suspension, and the approach roads to the turnpike were riddled with frost-heaves and potholes and ice. The winter had been hard. "It's like a goddam washboard," Jane said. Her voice was whiskey-thick, and he strained to hear her over the engine. "Like a roller coaster, Alex, can't you be careful for once?"

"I'm trying."

"Try harder," she said.

Suzanne slept, her blanket with its frayed silk edging up against her mouth. He saw all this in the rearview mirror—the threads responding to her breath, the rings on Jane's fingers and lace at her wrists, the golden cluster of his daughter's curls beneath her parka's hood. But he could not see the car seat; it was directly behind him. He could not turn sufficiently to see how Gillian fared. She made no sound, however; he collected his ticket at the turnpike entrance and turned east.

"I don't believe him," Jane announced.

"Why not?"

When drinking, she reverted to the insults of their youth. "He can't tell his ass from his elbow."

"Except he's the best we have. He himself suggested we go for a second opinion."

"To Mecca," she said. "Just because he trained there—Boston. The hell with it. He can't tell his ass from his elbow."

Alexander humored her. "Must make it hard for a surgeon."

"Ha ha," Jane said. "Mecca. The lame and the halt heading home."

Their families both hailed from Lexington, and therefore Boston did seem home; they would stay with her parents that night. Gillian had been an amiable infant—she stared and ate and slept as if at peace. At six months old, however, the pediatrician warned them that something was wrong with her legs. After consultation, she was placed in a Pavlik harness—trussed up like a portly frog so the ball would fit the socket of her dislocated hip. This had been difficult. They had had an anxious week till the buckles and straps became manageable; the Velcro tapes were urine-soaked, and Gillian complained. Soon enough, however, she learned to compensate; she crawled limp-legged across the flooring of their renovated barn. "'Man is born, he suffers and he dies,'" said Alexander, quoting Buddhist precepts that he did not deeply feel. "'There's worse to come as long as you can say that life's not over yet.'"

"That's chitchat," Jane said. "Just elegant chitchat. As long as they tell us our baby's all right . . ." She tilted the bottle toward him and left the phrase unfinished; Suzanne stirred in her sleep.

In Children's Hospital, however, the diagnosis was confirmed. Gillian would require an operation, and the sooner the better; she would wear a spica cast for six months at least.

This doctor was a woman; black-haired, wearing glasses. Her waiting room was full, and she had small interest in or patience with the Cullinans. "It's congenital," she said. "In ninety percent of the cases. And ninety percent of those affected are female. Did you"—she turned to Jane—"or did your mother have a dislocated hip?"

"Not that I know of," said Jane. "No one in our family."

"Well, there we have it then. The recessive gene." She took the X-rays once again and slapped them on a lighted screen. "We could admit her here," she said. "Or you could do it in Vermont. Go to the sixth floor and look at the ward. There's a baby there who's just been operated on, and the nurse will show you what it looks like. Good luck."

Dismissed, they rose. The baby on the sixth floor was stretched on a steel frame. She was encased in plaster from the armpits to the toes; the problem, the nurse said, was keeping the cast clean. Jane sat; she put her head down. "I'm dizzy," she said. "I may faint." There were rocking chairs and mobiles and stuffed animals on the ward; there were cuckoo clocks with sprung works on the walls. The child on the bed was logy from the anesthetic, said the nurse; she repeated the word "logy" as if, once alert, the child would have no cast. A plastic bag protruded, and there was a basin underneath the frame. "For her evacuations," the nurse said. She touched Alexander's arm, proprietary. "When she voids."

"We have to go now," Jane said.

Alexander held Gillian. She clutched her blanket, flush-faced, with the line of bone beneath her eyebrow pink from recent crying. "I have to have air," Jane said. "Thanks for the demonstration. We have to leave."

It was rush hour, and their retreat to Lexington was slow. In the car Jane keened; she rocked in her seat, saying, "Baby, my baby," and "Why did this happen to us?"

"It happened to her," he said. "It'll be better. She'll do the high jump."

"I want to die."

"You don't mean that."

"I do. I want this pain to end."

"It will."

"Six months. Six whole months in that cast. Just when she ought to be learning to walk. A toddler."

"She'll talk instead. I didn't walk, apparently, till I was two years old."

"You don't have to comfort me, Alex. You have a right to your own pain."

He braked. The traffic on Route 2 was heavy. "We'll make it."

"Of course. It takes two adults to turn her—that's what the nurse said." With her free hand she reached for his own. "It's torture, Alex. That cast."

"We'll manage," he assured her. "It could have been far worse."

In the days that followed, such assurance fled. The temperature dropped; he had to thaw their pipes one morning with a propane torch. It was minus thirty Fahrenheit, the worst cold snap on record for that week in February, and they huddled by the heat vents as if under siege. Alexander stayed home from the office and prepared his briefs under the eaves. Jane drank; he thought of himself as afflicted. Suzanne returned from the Early Childhood Center at two each afternoon, trudging in the tracks she'd made the week before; the snow was too heavy to shift. Alexander read fairy tales aloud. He fashioned paper crowns for her, and she danced to *The Nutcracker Suite*. Gillian would watch enchanted, banging her spoon on the tabletop. He fondled her continually, squeezing the flesh of her legs. On Tuesday she was admitted to the hospital, and Alexander drove to Albany, then flew through O'Hare to Moline; he had a claim to settle out of court. The John Deere company was willing to indemnify his client; their tractor's electrical system had exploded on ignition, and Sam Reed lost a leg.

"Mr. Cullinan," the farmer said, "they could give me five million. I'd take it, I ain't pretending I wouldn't. Between you and I. But they can't give me my leg."

Sam Reed was bald, with a white beard, and had provided maple syrup to the Cullinans for years. For Suzanne's first birthday, he had sent them a bushel of peas. He called up Alexander from a pay phone at the hospital, saying he could use help from an educated person in the law like you are, Mr. Cullinan. I know it's not the usual thing, but how would you feel with one foot on the pedal and one in the spreader all covered with shit; if he'd been alone that time he'd have bled to death in minutes. But they were putting him back together, Sam said, with pins and wire and plastic and soon enough he'd walk again, so what he wondered was what chance did a person stand of getting back at corporation presidents that never sat a tractor in their lives? Alexander said he'd help, and in the months that followed filed for damages. He deplaned in Moline in the snow.

"Can't you postpone it?" Jane had asked. "It's been dragging on for years."

"A year and a half. They're in a hurry."

"But can't you finish it by telephone? Of all the days we need you here . . ."

"I'll be back tomorrow, love. It's what Sam Reed's been dreaming of; it's not fair to ask him to wait."

"He's used to it. You're doing this for free, correct? So you want to get it over with; it's not like you're paid by the hour."

"Expenses," Alexander said. "We've got momentum now. Give them a change of venue or delay and they might change their minds."

He was proved right. The officials were conciliatory, generous; the facts of Mr. Reed's case having been ascertained, the depositions received, the faulty grounding located and the guarantee applicable because the intake-valve malfunction was not something they cared to make public, the John Deere company having a reputation to protect, and Mr. Reed having been unable to obtain redress from dealer or distributor, it devolved upon the company as such to compensate him for his leg. They were prepared so to do. They met Alexander at the airport and drove him to the offices and, over coffee, attained an agreement; by five o'clock the letters of intent were typed and signed.

He wanted to return. There was no plane, however, and the connection out of Cedar Rapids would be as efficient next morning; a company official who lived near Cedar Rapids offered to drive him there. Ned Sampson was insistent. It was the wrong way for Chicago but the right way for a drink; why not come home and eat with us, he asked, then book yourself out on the 7:05? Alexander had attended Columbia Law School while Ned was an undergraduate, and Ned thought the face looked familiar; the wife would love to meet you and we'll talk about old times.

Alexander refused. He said he was tired and needed some sleep; he explained about his daughter in the hospital. This excited Ned's strong sympathy; his secretary changed the booking and he would not hear of Alex having to eat out alone. They drove to Davenport, then Iowa City, in fog. The conversation flagged. There was a single lane carved out of the snow on I-80, and there were drifts. Ned Sampson lived on Summit Street; his driveway had been plowed. "Cost me thirty-five dollars this morning," he said. "For thirty yards and a turnaround. Should have bought a snowblower instead."

"Isn't it a long commute?"

"Mm-mn. But this town has some action in it, understand—a college town. It's where Alice comes from, besides."

Alice Sampson received them expansively. "I'm *so* glad you could come," she said. "I know what motel dinners must be like. And when Ned travels he's always so grateful for someone to talk to at night." Her palm was warm; she pressed his hand and held it, then turned as if in a square dance and, addressing the first partner, kissed her husband on the cheek. Her legs were good. "Where's Billy?" Ned asked.

"At the Parkers'," she said. "He wanted to sleep over, and I thought—when Sally called and said you'd be bringing Mr. Cullinan on down—I thought we might as well have us an evening alone." Her laugh was girlish, high. "And eat an *adult* supper for once. I do so want to hear about Ned's escapades in New York City way back when."

Alexander called the hospital. He reached Jane on the Pediatrics Ward. It was an hour later there, and Gillian had cried herself to sleep. "The traction's not so bad," she said. "It's a kind of stirrup, really, with weights. It's not so terrible. But everyone wears white in here, and every time she sees somebody wearing white she starts to cry."

"I don't blame her."

"They've taken blood. They take her temperature all the time. Suzy's all right. Dot's staying at the house, and they watched the Muppets. It's the cast that frightens me. I wish you were here."

"I will be tomorrow. We won. Sam Reed won't get five million, but he's got enough."

"Yes. Hurry."

"I'm taking the first plane," he said. "I'll be back just as soon as I can."

Ned brought him bourbon in a water glass. He took it soundlessly and drank. The walls of the study had photographs of Alice naked in a swimming pool, the water just under her breasts. Her eyes were closed, her hair was down; the breasts appeared to float. "Goodnight," he said to Jane. "I love you."

"Yes," she said. "I'm at the desk. The nurses here are friendly. Like riding a horse on your back."

"What?"

"The stirrups. It's one week in traction at least."

"I'll sleep there tomorrow. Warm up that bed."

"Yes. Goodnight."

"Kiss Gillian for me when she wakes up. Goodnight." He replaced the phone, stretched and drank. In the living room the lights were dim; James Galway played flute favorites, including "Annie's Song." Alice had her eyes closed and her head thrown back, as in the photographs; within the loose white blouse she wore, her breasts appeared less full. The couch was Naugahyde.

"You want to hear a story. You'll never believe this," said Ned. "When Lyndon Johnson quit—the night after his announcement—I was at a party. And I knew that we'd get Nixon then, somehow I knew it that night. So I was in a funk, understand, a real flat-out depression. And I went for a walk in Riverside Park, I mean nobody walks now in Riverside Park; it's dangerous at night. But things were different then, or maybe I just didn't care. And there was this yellow-haired thing, this midwestern beauty walking by the water too. Corn-fed. We didn't get busted or mugged, understand, I took her back to the party. Well, it's a simple story but the complicated thing, the part that makes it interesting and why I'm telling you, is this midwestern lady is my wife."

"Have another drink," she said.

The telephone rang. It was United Airlines calling to tell him his flight had been canceled; Ned's secretary had provided his home number. The fog was increasing; Cedar Rapids was shut and the equipment had been overflown. The storm had not yet reached Chicago, but snow was predicted; they could change his reservation for the day after; he had to decide. There would be surface transport available from Cedar Rapids to O'Hare at seven the next morning, but he would have to miss the flight for Albany, and the storm was heading east. Alexander tried to route himself through Minneapolis or Den-

ver, but the computer denied him; he could not leave from
Iowa except along the ground. Moline was also closed. If he
could reach O'Hare, United Airlines said, his morning flight
was listed routine, and Albany was clear. He said that he would
try to drive; the lady in Chicago advised him to drive carefully.
He thanked her and hung up.

"A problem?" Ned inquired.

"Yes. Are there car rentals in this town?"

"Out at the airport, maybe. Not in this village at night."

He called and got no answer. Alice brought him cheese.
The cheese was bite-size, with toothpicks protruding. She
loosened his tie for him, smiling. Her fingernails were pink.
"What about buses?" he asked. "Is there a Greyhound to
Chicago?"

"It's a local," Alice said. "You don't have to hurry."

"I do."

She studied him. "I'd like it if you stayed."

"I'd like it too. But there's a daughter in a hospital."

"Ned told me. I know."

"I've got to get home."

"Home." She repeated this without inflection, as if home
were a word that failed to signify. He did not know, and would
not, what her wide-armed welcome was intended to convey;
he imagined Gillian in fitful sleep, Jane drinking beside her,
and put down his glass.

"Where's the station?"

"Just around the corner," Ned announced. "Two rights,
the first left."

"I should have headed back this afternoon."

"I'm sorry."

"No. It's not your fault. You were being generous."

"I'll drive you to Chicago. Hell . . ."

Alexander wanted credit for his good behavior. He did
not wish to share or apportion such credit. "Just point me to
the bus."

*   *   *

The terminal was empty. There was a bearded man asleep
on a back bench, and a counter with a clock behind it, reading
8:15. There was bright fluorescent lighting, and the walls of the
room displayed framed posters of Biarritz. He had an hour to
wait. He settled down to do so, consigned to that limbo where
the traveler goes nameless and unrecognized, where no one
who knew him knew where they might find him. The paving
was slick. He had nearly fallen in the terminal's front lot.

When finally the bus arrived, it was eleven o'clock. The
driver took his money, said, "Them roads are like a skating
rink," and told him to go get a seat. There were none, it appeared. Then a black man on the aisle stirred in his sleep from
the sprawl that had taken two places, and Alexander sat. He
had, he realized, never ridden a long-distance bus in America;
he had done so with some frequency in Italy and Switzerland
and India and France. The dark shapes all around him seemed
inured to such slow passage; they were asleep, or talking softly
or staring out windows at Iowa City in fog. Smoking was for-
bidden; he would have welcomed a smoke. The bus, with its
windows sealed shut, felt overheated; he transferred his briefcase and satchel to the rack. Standing, he took off his overcoat
also; the bags were from a matched set Jane had given him on
his thirty-fifth birthday, with his initials underneath the MC
from Mark Cross. He felt embarrassed by such luxury and
grateful for the dark; the black man beside him shifted again,
his head shaved and skull like a mask. The eyebrows had a
ridge of bone, and Alexander spent some minutes trying to
identify the face; his father had instructed him in the distin-
guishing marks of masks. The phrase "Yoruba, Ibo, Dan" became the litany of remembrance, and he decided that his
neighbor derived from Ibo stock.

His father had had a collection of masks, and Alexander
used to brandish shields and spears and daggers in the living
room. His favorite mask was Ekoi and trimmed with human

skin. "It's possible," his father said. "The skin here could be antelope. But that's thicker, usually, and not so mottled. These teeth are monkey teeth."

They stopped at a motel in order to change drivers, then stopped at Davenport. He closed his eyes but could not sleep, saw Gillian encased in plaster, Sam Reed blown apart. The fog was thick; the turnpike lights had a soft yellow nimbus, and he heard the trucks they passed before he saw them looming. The driver wiped his windshield often, but there was no snow.

Alexander read signs to Wisconsin and to Indiana; they reached the outskirts of Chicago before dawn. Then the traffic increased. At six o'clock the sky had not cleared, and he commenced to worry that O'Hare would also close. Arrived at the Greyhound Terminal, he called United Airlines, and the operator said the equipment was in Chicago, but that the decision to fly would be taken at departure time; he confirmed his booking, and she said, "Good luck." He drank from a child's water fountain, then took the escalator up to find a taxi for O'Hare.

At the top of the escalator, a crate with wire strapping blocked his path. It occupied the width of the platform. He hurdled the thing and fell free. The act of leaping gave him pleasure, he walked with loose-legged jauntiness past the janitor who watched. A policeman waved his nightstick at a woman wearing hot pants and yellow platform shoes; there were rows of travelers watching TV. At seven o'clock the outside air had a wet chill; he breathed this with relief. Two men approached him and lunged for his bags, crying, "Airport, sir?"

"All right," he said. "How much?"

The younger one was jumpy; his taxi was the first in line. "Get in, get in."

"How much to O'Hare?"

"I'll drive you, sir." He wrenched open the passenger door and revealed a body; he pulled the man out by the feet. His speech shifted accent; he came from the islands. "Out wid

you, mon, out I say." The man within unfolded. He was stag-
gering-drunk, six foot six at least. His eyes were yellow; his
forehead was cut and there was dried blood on the wound. He
steadied himself on Alexander's shoulder, then spun off. "Get
in, get in. Twenty dollars."

Alexander turned. The elder driver smiled at him, retreat-
ing to the second car. He did not know the proper price but
felt compelled to bargain. "Twenty dollars is too much."

"The book, the book! That's what it say in the book for the
airport."

"Show me."

The driver flipped through pages and produced a suburb
called Des Plaines. "Twenty dollars to Des Plaines, that's what
it cost. It the rules."

"O'Hare," said Alexander. "I don't want to go to Des
Plaines." He entered the second cab, hearing cries of "Fifteen
dollars! Twelve! I take you, sir," and settled in. The second
driver laughed. "He tried to fool you, see, it don't take twenty
dollars. Not to O'Hare. Fifteen's more like it, sir. He look in the
book and you look in the book, and there's no airport where
he looking. You a person who *travels,* correct?"

"Correct."

"That boy he don't know nothing. He thought he could
fool you. Des Plaines!"

The fog was palpable. Alexander closed his eyes. The
driver was solicitous; he lectured Alexander on the need to get
some rest. He himself came from Natchez but worked in Chicago and had his children and grandchildren in Chicago also;
that was what was keeping him when he could go home. He
had a pension from the railroad and he drove this taxi for
diversion and because the times were tight; just to keep busy,
understand, keeping out of his wife's hair. He asked where
Alexander was going, and when Alexander said Albany, he
asked if Alexander lived near the Rockefeller ranch. They discussed the death of Nelson Rockefeller, and the driver specu-

lated on the role of Nelson's wife and brothers, how much money they would get and what he himself would have done with the money; he reminded Alexander that Joe Kennedy left more behind than Rockefeller, four hundred million to sixty-six about, and he wondered whether maybe someone could be holding something back; he wasn't a fisherman himself but he could smell something fishy like that a mile off and driving a cab. He asked what was Alexander doing in this town, and whether he had family, and when he learned the reason for the trip he said, God bless your daughter and don't worry she'll be fine. They drove in silence then. The airport was crowded; he had forty minutes to spare before his scheduled flight. When Alexander proffered a five-dollar tip, the cabbie repeated, "God bless you. I'll pray for your daughter. Good luck."

He called his home. Suzanne answered. "Who is it?"

"Hi, darling."

"*Hi,* Daddy."

"How are you?"

"Fine." She said this with an intonation she reserved for phones—languorous and sweetly thoughtful. "I miss you."

"I miss you."

"When will you be coming back?"

"As soon as possible. I'm on my way. Almost there. How were the Muppets?"

"Fine." She would not be deflected. "Tonight? To-morrow?"

"Today, I hope. Is Mommy at the hospital?"

"Yes. Do you want to speak to Dot?"

"I just called to wish you good morning. You're off to school now?"

"Yes."

"I'm glad to hear your voice," he said. "I'm bringing you a present."

She hugged the phone. She told him she was hugging it, then promised she would build a snowman after school. It would be at the top of the driveway, she said, it would be the first thing he would see.

His plane was late. O'Hare had one functional runway for arrivals and one for departures; the problem was not fog so much as ice. He bought a motorized Snoopy for Suzanne, perfume for Jane and a tin of cigars for himself. He bought a newspaper and tried to read; he consulted the departure screen frequently and drank two Bloody Marys at the stand-up bar. The Midwest was an obstacle course he was trying to negotiate; his skills were those of motion and not immobility. The man beside him serviced a high-speed paper counter, and he said the competition was seeking an injunction—in eighteen months he had them running scared. He'd worked for a firm out of England until just eighteen months ago when he'd started up his own. He'd quit when he was good and ready and not because some candyass English assholes asked him to cease and desist.

The captain welcomed them. He said the field conditions in Albany were such that the decision to land there would be taken on approach. He apologized for the delay and hoped they'd have a pleasant flight. The flight attendants would be bringing breakfast as soon as they were airborne, and he'd announce their destination just as soon as possible; they were number seven on the runway for departure.

The plane rumbled forward. He watched the processional—planes at right angles rolling to position, then the sudden check and halt and accelerating release. He studied his hands. The plane roared, immobile. He remembered his first flight—to Washington, with his father who took him along for the sheer sport and spectacle, the cloud bank beneath them seeming like swansdown, the tilt and rise of it and his stomach lurching with each updraft and descent. He thought of Robin

Templeton in college, and his army training plane; the best thing for a hangover, Robin used to claim, the only way to clear your brain is try a few maneuvers. So they would go up in the morning after parties, boasting of the night before or the antic-ipated night to come, and Alexander would strap himself in, his head a riot of panicky pride, the taste of metal in his mouth while Robin looped the loop.

His mother's dying wish had been to have her ashes spread on some loved stretch of countryside. She had been cremated, and Alexander took the urn. He chartered a Coman-che out of the Bennington airport, and the pilot flew for half an hour over the Green Mountains till the fields beneath them seemed mere shape and the hills and lakes and villages went unrecognized. Then Alexander opened the door, work-ing the urn cap loose and scattering ash. He had not antici-pated the force of the wind, or the door's resistance, and much of the bone and ash flew back inside the plane. He held the urn, however, letting air empty it out. Much of the ash, he told himself, would surely have been coffin-ash, and the bone had been transformed to the size and consistency of cat litter. He took a shower later, washing this substance out of his hair, until the hot water was gone.

"We're number two in line now, folks," the pilot said. "Will flight attendants take their positions."

Alexander thought of how he'd learned to ride, to set his horse at a canter by pulling back on the reins, then kicking at the instant of release. Jane was the better rider, on the more spirited horse, and she would bolt in front of him, raising dust or mud. They lifted free. He felt the now familiar tilt and rise. The flight was smooth. They could not land at Albany, how-ever, and landed at Plattsburgh instead. He had been traveling now for twenty-seven hours, and the airline bus to Albany would take him too far south. He went to the information counter and asked, "You got a boat?"

"Sir?"

"I've been in a car," he said. "And bus and taxi and plane. I require a boat now."

"Sir?"

"To bring this trip full circle. My car's locked anyhow. It's in the long-term parking lot at Albany. I'll leave it there. My daughter's in the hospital."

"I'm sorry, sir." The woman at the information counter assessed him, uncertain. "Where were you planning to go?"

He told her. She suggested Amtrak, and he took a taxi to the Amtrak station. The subsequent hours unreeled in slow motion, and all he would retain were frames: blurred, indistinct, himself jolting backward through snow. His baby lay in a hospital bed; he would tell her on arrival, though she would not comprehend him, how the world is in an orbit and all things are therefore circular.

At Saratoga Springs he disembarked. There were no taxis waiting, and he watched the train head south. Here the cold was absolute, and he waited by the train tracks for a taxi to arrive. There was a work crew on a siding, spreading calcium to clear the track. They dug and shoveled and ladled the stuff thickly on a single rail. Alexander raised his collar and watched his breath condense. He faced the four directions, turning slowly and counting to ten; he tried to imagine himself as a compass, the fixed point where Gillian lay conjoined to all such circling. She would improve. They would manage. The three men leaned on their shovels. They watched him till he turned their way and then returned to work.

OSTINATO

December 12

Dear Mr. Bentham:

    I hope you and Mrs. Bentham are having a pleasant winter in Truro. How I wish to be there with you to spend summer the same way I spent it in the past with both of you. For when I think about you and your place I always get a special feeling, the feeling you get for special places and people you have loved and trusted and found happiness with once, just like the feeling I get toward my home in Japan and to my family.

    I just come back from the concert hall. I give exact information about your performance to the all of my friends because it gives me a sheer pleasure, Mr. Bentham, of being your friend that I always feel so proud of. Yes to tell the truth I wanted ticket to send Jon as a gift.

It's sound romantic, isn't it? And I think I am, as I were sometimes. Anyway I have already invited him for your concert because I wanted him to meet you and I wanted you to meet him because I like him a lot and I like you a lot. Also, to me it is the only chance to ask him openly to be with me and it is the only chance he can accept the concert in a casual way. So would you please meet him for me? I met him at the Pub Club where he was playing piano as a member of the young music band. And there was no special relationship between us except he as a music player and singer and I as a one of fan among the many of his fan, at least I made it clear to him and myself. And I think he understand it.

But it's me who failed again in a game of love. Problem is that when I become to like someone I could not play it as I should. I play it too seriously, I think. That's why it hurts me now when we see each other like stranger again though my feeling toward him are still same. It is foolish to feel hurt when I know the reason why I was attracted to him is only that he is so beautiful and charming and young, 26 years old, and although he care for me enough to come up to my table on a recess whenever I go there sometimes, half of it are out of courtesy. And I wish we were once lovers and strangers again the next morning rather than purely platonic. And worse of all we are not even in platonic love either. Yet I can't ignore him.

Anyway, he will be gone again soon and we might not see each other anymore. So I would like to make a last chance of togetherness with him and first reunion in five years with you to be a perfect one. So please help me make it wonderful one for three of us. That means I would like to have pleasant night with most smile and laughter that is only possible between true friends if we can only see you for a few moment at the backstage after concert. But I wish we could find some time to talk. He is young but not like hippies although he has a long hair but it is beautiful so he won't make you feel any embarrassment. That's I can promise about him.

By the way what time will you arrive here on Monday? If you are not tired and don't mind to listen to the music they play which I am afraid you might say that it is not music but loud noise unless you find it something personally attractive, and personally I think

*they play pretty well, I am mostly happy to come to his place with you.
In any case please write me as how I can see you if you have still got
a time but if not please call as soon as you are in Halifax. And please
leave a message if I was not in. Although I will be careful not to miss
your telephone all day.*

*I wish you safe trip. Again I wish Mrs. Bentham will be here too
so you will help me with my trouble and then everything will be
settled in nicest way.*

See you soon. P.S. I enclose telephone and address. In hastly.

Mishiko

"Well?"

"Well what?"

"Are you going to see her?"

"What do you want me to do?"

"How long has it been?" Helen asked. She gave the letter
back to him, and he left it on the table.

"Five years," Richard said."I would have thought she'd be
in Tokyo again."

"Nara."

"Tokyo was where she worked, remember?"

"I wouldn't remember."

"Come off it, Helen. You do."

"Yes. I suppose so. There's so much to remember."

He paused. "Her visa—working papers. They must have
been renewed."

"She found some other happy family. Some other cultural
exchange program."

"I don't have to see her," Richard said.

"She'll find you, anyhow. Those hands of yours will be
caressing keys on every lamppost in Halifax. Has she written
before?"

"No."

"'*Mr.* Bentham,' it says. Only 'Mr. Bentham.' She could
have included us both."

"I'm the one who's going, right? She's got another pianist."

"Younger this time."

He looked at his hands. "Not so famous."

"No. Not yet, at any rate. That's why she wants you to meet him."

"A rock 'n' roll band? She wants me to listen to some third-rate pianist at the, what's it called . . . ?"

"The Pub Club," Helen said.

"Yes. Why don't you come with me?"

"No."

"Please. I could use the protection."

"You're dying to meet them. Her. Anyhow, it's the most beautiful month here."

He pocketed the letter. "Why don't you join me for once?"

"No."

"Just overnight? There's a darling little pub club."

"Please. I don't want to talk about it. You know I can't come."

He changed his tone. "I never really know, now do I? What's so marvelous about December here alone?"

"The privacy," she said.

"We'll miss Christmas together. You wouldn't have to leave the hotel."

"It isn't overnight. It's the first in a series of concerts—two weeks."

"You could come back." He raised his hands. "But have it your way, Helen."

"Don't wheedle. *You're* the one who booked this tour." She said this with the intonation he had used before—a practiced self-pity soliciting praise. "It's your way too. Ours."

"She was a good gardener. You said so yourself."

"Snow peas," Helen said. "On those tender little knees of hers, picking up the weeds with her fingers like tweezers. One by one. So terribly attractive."

"She did help with the house."

"She's crazy if she thinks I'll have her back."

"She doesn't think that."

"So find out what she does think. What she's after. Go to her."

"I'm going to Halifax, remember? Not to her."

"The Oriental mysteries. A massage parlor for the maestro's fingers. 'Oh, please, Mr. Bentham,'" she mimicked, "'let me chop the callots. Don't hurt your hands.'"

"All right."

"It's not all right."

"I can't cancel."

"No, I know that, darling. You couldn't help it, could you?"

"If she wants to come," he said, "I'll see her. But I won't try to find her."

"It's a flee countly," said Helen. "You do what's best to do."

That week he drove to Boston, trying to assess the winter colors of the Cape. His windshield was tinted, and the sky's blue had depth. The pine trees were less green than in the summertime, and the sand less brilliant at the edges of Route 6. He wondered, as often before, if Mishiko had been truly displaced or would seem at home in Tokyo. There, he imagined, she'd know her directions—knowing in the signless streets which way to turn for the theater or where to purchase fish. He made the plane at Logan with little time to spare, carrying his music in his briefcase. His itinerary looked this month, he'd joked, like a primer course in foolishness: name sixteen towns you've never heard of, and Richard Bentham will be there, introducing Eskimos to Bach.

It had been more disconcerting than he'd dared acknowledge. He had not seen her handwriting in years. The perfectly wielded pen, the black precision of her script stood in such

startling contrast to the mutilated language as to appear nearly
purposive—as if she mocked his exactness by both aping and
burlesquing it. Or as if she'd wanted, after all this time away, to
show that she'd learned nothing since she departed their
house. Or as if she wrote him in an agreed-on code—but one
that he'd forgotten how to read.

Yet there remained her habitual grace. He'd not been
wrong in urging her to make a career of transcribing; there
were few enough by now that you could trust with scores.
Instead—what was she doing?—receiving unemployment,
probably, in some backwater street in some town in Nova
Scotia. He ordered bourbon, neat, and sat back and kicked off
his shoes.

More and more successful, he'd been less and less at
home these years. A performing career has its own sort of
logic, he'd say; you play until they stop inviting you. At first,
and even when they could barely afford it, Helen traveled with
him. She delighted in the bustle and applause. While he practiced in the windy halls, gauging the piano's action, she would
roam whatever place they'd come to, finding the museums or
shopping arcades or bistros or fountains that later, alone, he
would never quite manage to find. She would acquire scarves
or catalogues or pastry or the region's wine. Then they'd meet
at the hotel at three. They would shower and nap and make
love, his mind empty of all but that preparatory hush he
needed for the sounding silence of the concert yet to come.

Things changed. Helen grew more needy but appeared to
need him less. They bought a summer house in Truro and had
it winterized. They kept their rent-controlled apartment in
New York, and she began referring to it as their West Side
pied-à-terre. She painted—badly, he thought. She took Yoga
and dance and recorder lessons. Impatient with any but dem-
onstrated expertise or professional ambitions, Richard found
himself humoring her. They had no children. In what they
agreed was a predictable seven-year crisis, Helen said, "It's just

too much. Keeping the home fires burning. I do need help with the place."

So he found the thirty-year-old cousin of the daughter of his recording engineer: a Japanese. They sponsored her arrival and guaranteed employment. They fetched her at Logan—a pale, mute person wearing jeans, with two straw suitcases she'd tied together at the handles. That summer, he had promised Helen, he would stay at home. And with the exception of a master class or two, with the exception of recording dates in Amsterdam and the festival at Bath, he did remain in Truro. He was, he told himself, attempting to shore up collapse.

They painted the house. He heard somewhere that Jung had cured a patient by telling him to stop analysis and purchase an acre of land. So he had truckloads of topsoil delivered, and they staked out a garden on the southern slope. City people, the Benthams were clumsy at first, but he reveled in the amateurish frenzy of it—cutting stakes for fence posts and digging and forking and hoeing with such glad abandon that Helen feared for his hands.

The flight was rough; Richard stared at the clouds. Mishiko had been patient, practiced, and she tended the garden with care. She liked to do the marketing, and she cleaned their spattered paint. They gave her a portable radio for her birthday. She acquired a broad-brimmed straw hat also, and would accompany them to the beach, sitting in her own created shade with earphones, nodding. For her sojourn in the garden, she would turn the volume up. "It frightens the rabbits," she said. Later, when he pictured her, it was always in that hat, on her knees in front of the pole beans or corn, being crooned at by some caterwauling indecipherable Englishmen, rapt.

He would emerge from his day's practice, blinking in the sun. The two of them would greet him—Helen dark and seeming heavy by comparison. He would propose a sail or swim, and they would proffer the harvest, and Mishiko would turn down the sound. She seemed like some ancient retainer or servingwoman to him then—three steps behind him where they walked, a gliding presence perfectly located in their lives. When Helen left for New York—to see her doctor, she said, and to deal with the rubble that the upstairs tenant's overflowing bathtub had made of their dining room ceiling—it seemed merely proper that he enter the guest room bed.

Mishiko accepted him. A woman, he maintained, should take off modesty with her clothes. Yet she was clothed in passionate demureness for the nights that they made love. In the morning she served him tea and buttered toast, the radio already on, as if nothing could have altered the pattern set up that June. She left the following week. He acquiesced in her departure with relief. Though she'd become his mistress, she attempted to explain, Helen was still mistress of the house.

December 22

Dear Mrs. Bentham:

I can't tell you enough how glad and happy I was to seeing Mr. Bentham again. On Monday we had few hours to talk and laugh together as we used to did and I can't believe that there is five years between us to meet again. I can picture it clearly when Mr. Bentham says that "everything is same in Truro," even though I have heard all news, including the some of sad news that had happened to the people I knew of. But back to the first night I must tell you that, in spite of Mr. Bentham's busy schedule, it was so nice to accept my wish to come and see my "wish-to-be-my-boyfriend" and I was so happy with seeing two man-friend I like so much talking together. However, in spite of Mr. Bentham's cooperation, it was I think the night I had really put Jon into difficult situation and made him really hate me. If I hadn't a pleasant time with Mr. Bentham I would have been so unhappy and depressed for the result of coming to the concert with Dave instead of Jon. Yet I am glad whole situation seems turned out very nicely for every one. The concert was beautiful as always, and Dave, my former employer who gave me the first job in Canada to do airbrushing on T-shirt and I still work for him occasionally when he needs, enjoyed it immensely and Grace, who was my roommate and nice friend, enjoyed it too.

There was another enjoyable time when Mr. Bentham took me to the Japanese restaurant. It was a restaurant I worked as a cashier for four weeks in September. There it was snowing. I must thank you again for most pleasant time. One thing I regret myself is I failed to call Mr. Bentham this morning to say one more time "Thank you" and "Good-bye" and "Wishing you a nice trip," etc. I called all right but it was too late. Hotel-man said that he left five minutes ago. I called two airline to find out if . . . but by the time I find out right airline I give up to call because I thought it might give Mr. Bentham a only trouble to get it if he was not nearby telephone.

I do hope Mr. Bentham will be continuing safe trip with successful musical performance. And I do hope you will not be too lonely while Mr. Bentham is away and not be too tired or bored. Love.

Mishiko

The mystery, of course, was how she had stood it at all—not how she had withstood it for so long. Her grandmother had turned one hundred in November. Helen journeyed to the nursing home and attended a party the other inmates—she couldn't help it, she thought of them as inmates—put on. They had ice cream and cake and party hats and favors, and her grandmother wore a corsage. When the singing was over her grandmother stood and clattered on her water glass for attention. She looked so prim but nervous that Helen by her side had straightened also, straining. Then she delivered a speech. In her singsong, high-pitched whisper, the celebrant said, "Life is not what you make it. Life is how you take it," and fell back to her chair as if released.

Ths jingle stayed with Helen through the holidays. She found herself repeating it in front of the news, or while drinking coffee, or in the intervals she paced by her easel, considering a Wyeth-like series of gulls. She heard no music those weeks. Richard's records bulked beneath the stereo system like a dusty, pinched reproach; he'd made so many lately that the space she allocated to her husband could scarcely contain him. She put out suet and sunflower seed. The chickadees and jays and grosbeaks clustered to her feeders, and she watched them through the picture windows, unafraid. When Mishiko's letter arrived on December 24, she called Bill up to wish him Merry Christmas, and to ask if there were some sort of party she might attend or make. He said, "But gladly, gladly," and came down from Provincetown that night with a bottle of Old Bushmills. She had had trouble with the fireplace, and he pointed out to her—gently, not making it a joke or an occasion for scorn—that first she had to open the flue. Then he built a fire, mixing in pitch pine and oak and warming the living room so that they elected to lie down in front of it, no other lights on in the house.

Bill stroked her back. He blundered on about the possibility of change, how she could come with him to Provincetown and maybe San Miguel de Allende, where he taught in the Art Institute, and he'd show her turkey buzzards to sketch instead of gulls. "*Xopilotes*," Bill said. "That's what they call them there." The mystery was how to make the world of art and privilege seem anything but grown-up games, be born again, was how to pry free his fingers as they closed upon her arm. Bill said she kindled flame in him, but Helen fell asleep. She heard the language of seduction go up the chimney, weightless, incorporeal as smoke.

When Richard called the next morning, she told him that a family of pheasants had settled by the junipers beyond the porch. That seemed the most important thing; she had nothing to ask or report. He said, "It's hard to be apart," and she agreed. He said, "I wish you'd come with me," and she answered, "Yes. That would be nice." He told her that he'd be back home the following Sunday by eight.

She read the Sunday *Times*. She left *The Tale of Genji* with a bookmark in it by their bed. She wondered if the nastiness that had invaded her these months (the word for it *was* nastiness, this chill propriety and prejudice she'd thought of as her mother's curse) might dissipate and lift. She made a New Year's resolution that such brittle rigor would go. The problem was just how to make it go. The issue was where to locate that shivering delight she'd known at twenty or thirty or even last year when listening to Richard perform the *Schubert Impromptus.* Or in some tavern with him, dancing in a circle dance with sweaty men with handkerchiefs; the question was where pleasure fled and hid.

Helen studied herself in the mirror. It was not unkind. The flesh that had been soft was firm, the planes of her face more pronounced. She dressed herself attentively, pulled out but did not play his record of the *Goldberg Variations,* and settled in to wait. She made canapés. The few cars passing by their house seemed self-propelled and pilotless; their headlights lit the pine trees at the driveway's end.

Then Richard arrived. He rumbled down the driveway and she heard his brakes complain. She listened to him, motionless, hearing the engine roar and cease, hearing him open the car door, then the trunk. She heard him stamp and shuffle up the steps she had remembered to light, and opened the front door in for him as he opened the storm door out. The mystery was how he did not notice, as she greeted and embraced him and took off his overcoat, how she'd traveled so far to return.

"Welcome, world traveler," she said. He said the house looked lovely, and so did its mistress, his wife.

After he'd unpacked, given her the perfume and a Hudson's Bay blanket (blue, with a dark blue stripe, and doubling the size of his luggage and anyhow not as good as blubber for igloos, he said), after she'd told him that seals were in the harbor here, and asked about the audience in Montreal, the cousin who came to Toronto to hear him, told about the New

Year's celebration where they'd gotten so falling-down drunk that William pretended the dunes were a ski slope, and said the Witherecks were sweet, had been utterly insistent that she dine with them, two times, and that she'd therefore asked them to dinner on Monday, tomorrow, and hoped he didn't mind; after she'd asked for and seen his reviews, complimented his haircut, asked about the weather in Vancouver and said they did have snow for Christmas but it didn't last, she brought out cheese and rum and said, "I got her letter."

"Whose?"

"Hers. About the nights in Halifax."

"Oh. Mishiko's."

"Yes. Mishiko's."

"And what did she tell you?" he asked.

Then Helen stretched and watched him watching her; her breasts rose with the motion and she locked her hands behind her head, leaned back.

"Do you want to see the letter?"

"Not especially. Not yet."

"Her grammar's no better," she said. "It must have been some scene."

"What?"

"The nightclub. The boyfriend. The three of you wrestling."

"Do we have to discuss this?"

"No."

"I'll have another drink, then."

She covered her glass with her palm. "No, thanks. Not yet. I want to discuss it."

"Oh, Helen . . ."

"Oh, Helen, what?"

Richard sighed. He topped his drink and watched the liquid rise above the level of the glass. It adhered to itself, and he hunted the word for such molecular adherence.

"Oh, Helen, *what?*" she repeated.

Meniscus—that was it; he drank, pleased. "Oh, Helen, I've just gotten here. So let's not squabble over lunatics, all right?"

"Like who?"

"Like those two. Cheers. Your health."

"To us," she said. "Someone cut a blue spruce from the driveway. I'd been to Provincetown shopping, and I'd anyhow decided not to buy a tree this year. But up there by the parking lot I noticed something missing. And I knew it right away—the spruce that you planted, the middle one—the best. We've got a wreath on the door. It doesn't seem fair."

"I'll talk to the police."

"For what? Because they cut a Christmas tree? He never made your concert, did he?"

"Jon? No. But Dave did, and the airbrush gang."

"You spent *two* nights with her."

"The first at the nightclub, the second at the concert hall. We called."

"Not very often."

"Often enough. You weren't home."

"Look, is this some sort of inquisition?"

"I rather thought it was," said Richard.

She stretched again. He had the menace of strangeness about him, always, after such trips. She set herself to elicit his threatless familiarity. "I do like that haircut," she said. "Where did you get it?"

"The airport. I can't remember which one now. Somewhere we had to wait."

"I did cry, darling. About that tree. I stood there with my groceries, watching the place where the sap still leaked, just feeling so sorry for us . . ."

"There are enough trees," he said.

"I'll go with you next tour, maybe. To France?"

"Yes. And Italy. It would be fine."

"Yes."

"I'll tell you what her letter said," he said. "If there's anything else then she lied. I got to Halifax that evening, and got to the hotel. She was there; she'd been waiting by the desk all day, she told me, but it didn't matter, she was pleased to find the right one. Grinning, speechless. She wondered if I'd go to the Pub Club—hear her little rinky-dink ragtime pianist, Jon. I think they called themselves the Wolverines. Yes. Bishop and the Wolverines. That's what they called themselves. Jon Bishop. From Ireland, can you beat it? A Bishop?"

"They're Catholic there," Helen said.

"Well, anyway, we went."

"You don't have to tell me."

"I know. That's why I'm doing it. He must have been appalled to see me—this ancient, earnest person come to check on his intentions. Stride piano, that's what he played. Not all that badly either, I have to give him that. And Mishiko just sat there, nodding, beaming, drinking milk, and he joined us between sets. We talked about Rachmaninoff. He'd learned the name to impress me, I think, but he said he always thought Rachmaninoff was the nuts."

"He didn't!" Helen laughed.

"Yes. He used that expression—the nuts. So I agreed with him but said that I believed Fats Waller was just the nuts also, and Willie Smith, and we discussed the respective merits of Rachmaninoff and Waller and Willie 'The Lion' Smith. Then I paid and said I had to get some sleep and thanked him. Said I hoped he'd come to my concert tomorrow, and left them there, and left."

"We're being condescending."

"Yes."

"He didn't come."

"No."

"What did he look like?"

"Red-headed," Richard said. "A Vandyke beard, more or less. Short and thick and wearing sequins and one earring. Just her type."

"It doesn't matter."

"There's more."

"No more. You're home again and have a haircut and it's the New Year. Later you can tell me," Helen said.

"Next day I took her out to lunch. To the restaurant she'd worked at—a kind of Horn and Hardart's, where you could eat *sashimi*. Rice. *Sukyaki* for a dollar; it was awful."

"Is she happy?" Helen asked.

"I wouldn't be."

"That's not my question. Is she?"

"Would you be? With so little?"

Richard gestured at the tasseled rugs, and at the marsh outside. He turned on the floodlights and it seemed as if they saw the bay, down beyond the flagstone path: boats raised on blocks at the edge of the visible, all they surveyed and owned. She spread out their thick new blanket.

"I want to be happy," said Helen. "It's my New Year's resolution."

"Yes."

"Do please take your shoes off. I'm trying."

"Yes."

He did, and she embraced him and felt him rise against her. The contours of their flesh fused in practiced opposition. Richard lay on top of her, and she on the Hudson's Bay blanket. But as their bodies meshed she felt such unslaked hunger for some further kind of fusion that she wept; she could not halt the crying that he took as love's approval and excited him; he plunged inside her fiercely while she formulated words like "condescension"; "Murasaki"; "sea." She tried to make a pattern of them, but they would not scan; she tried to find a rhythm in them, but they did not fit. Her husband's weight was as an anchor; it kept them together yet kept them apart. He stood. He said, "I love you," and transferred his clothes to the hamper. She was not endangered, not adrift.

January 8

Dear Mr. and Mrs. Bentham:

I have finally got the photograph to be developed and enlarged, and I am very happy to be sending you now. I hope you would love it as much as I do. You and Jon looks so gorgeous in the picture. This is the first time in my life I get complete satisfaction out of pictures I have ever possessed. I would cherish it and admire it always and every time I look at it I will remember all the beautiful memories those beautiful people, you and Jon, have brought to me.

I regret to say that the pictures taken at the backstage on the night of your concert has been all come out black which I was half suspected since the flashlight did not work normally then. For that picture I hope there will be another chance again, possibly next year when you are here?

There is one more thought for which I also need your help for securing a job. I would like work as stagehand or paint stage props at a theater. What I am hoping for is your influential assistance to get some steady connections with people in theater management. Since you are performing I thought you have access to the people even though yours is a musical society. I was tempted to apply for it here but I dare not try because I know the results before start. If I apply for it all by myself because I would never get the job when at mere sight of me the interviewer will say that it is not a woman's job. I do hope you have someone in mind who can help.

By the way I would like to tell about the letter I had received from Jon. It was a letter of apology and he explained in it that he sent his apologies to the theater to you backstage about 8 o'clock on concert night. I don't know if you really receive it or not.

Whether what he is saying is true or not please forgive him for what he meant to. He has left for his home country after his last performance. He will be coming back in April and will be playing 6 weeks from 5th of April and maybe in May too. Ever since he left to his home in Ireland he has sending me nice letter explaining why he had to acted with me like he had been. I think we will remain as a best friend for each other for the rest of our life since it is the best and only way we could find our happiness. I think we both know there will be no other way. Now he says he is going to send me a record which will be released soon. That is all we are now at the moment. I am also sending him a picture, and I am happy.

Mishiko

MARCHING
THROUGH
GEORGIA

He arrived in Knoxville half asleep, having left for Albany at five. The trip was uneventful though prolonged. There was rain at the Albany airport, then rain at Islip and Washington; the skies cleared while he waited for his connecting flight. His lecture was scheduled for four.

George Allison liked travel; it gave him some sense of expanse. But he had done enough of it these months, he told his wife, to last a year. She had kissed him sleepily. "Be careful." Allyn stood at the door. "Don't step on any alligators."

"No. Go back to bed."

"Wish you were here," Allyn said.

His taxi driver had been garrulous. "I'm glad you asked me, Professor. I wouldn't want you driving down yourself. The way they keep the airport parking lot. It ain't safe. I hate to think of you leaving that sports car behind."

"I'll just be gone three days," George said. "But it isn't worth the hubcaps."

"Hubcaps, hell," said Billy Peck. "They'd take the tires too."

George made no answer. The autumn dawn was cold. They were driving in the limousine that Billy Peck used for funerals. The road was slick; they saw few cars. "I got to do a burial later," Peck said. "How's the family?"

"They're fine."

"The twins. I see them on the way to school."

"They're growing up," said George. In his raincoat, he shifted. It came as no surprise to know how much the driver knew, but it embarrassed him that he could not reciprocate. He did not know, for instance, if Billy Peck had married and had children of his own; it seemed too late to ask.

"I remember," Billy said, "when every night before we'd dig we'd burn a tire to draw up the frost. Speaking of tires. Just douse and light them is all. Sucks it right out of the ground. The supervisor used to tell us, save your tires, boys. Six foot of frost. They all used to do it . . ."

"What happened?"

"The way rubber smells. Pollution." In the light from the dashboard he examined his finger. "Outlaw this and outlaw that and now you dig graves you get a jackhammer to do it. Like working your way through concrete. You leave your car at airports and it's wrecked. Welfare benefits. But burn your own leaves and you're risking a fine." Billy chewed a cuticle. "A field full of tires, smoking," he said. "It's twenty years since I seen tires like that."

At the luncheon that they gave for him, George fought the desire to sleep. They discussed the inflation rate; the Chairman of the History Department sent regrets. His wife was in the hospital, they said; he would have been here otherwise, he'll be sorry to have missed it and he wants to hear the tape. They ate at the Faculty Club. His host, Sam Hall, was a previous acquaintance; as far back as college, Sam told the others, the two of them agreed to disagree. As far as he, Sam, was concerned it did a person honor to have George as his adversary. They discussed the siege of Vicksburg at some length.

The waiter brought him coffee. "Thank you very much," George said. The waiter seemed surprised. It would come at some point on the trip, it always did, and George accepted it now. Not so specific as shame, it nonetheless afflicted him—this sense of being welcome under false pretense. He was a fake, he told himself, not the smiling soft-voiced notable they waited for at airports and advanced on, threatless, hands held out. The hospitality was real. The local newspaper would have carried a three-year-previous photograph and a caption announcing his attainments; the campus radio station would have done the same. They did not know his work. They would misspell his name. But the intention was there, and the attention flattered him; Sam Hall had made his students read George's monograph on Grant. "I believe this summer we'll be heading north," Sam announced. "If they're still racing horses, we'll visit your part of the world."

The talk was a success. He presented his reading of Sherman: that the methodology of pacification derived from Caesar and presaged Ho Chi Minh. "A house divided against itself" is more a metaphor than faulty building technique; we may give Lincoln marks for diction but Sherman penned the deeper truth that "War is hell." In the discussion period, later, he displayed what was by now a characteristic blend of erudition and modesty; he lingered with the graduate students; he asked for permission to light his pipe. In the rest-room mirror he saw a stranger smiling back at him: the visitor, half drunk with lack of sleep and dizzy with recurrence. He called his home. The phone was busy; he told the operator he would try again.

They ate supper at a warehouse transformed into a restaurant; George had invited the Halls. The decor was a cross between Gay Nineties, Gashouse and French Brothel; a red
lantern hung above their table. Ginny Hall was pink and
plump, excited by her first night out in what she said was
weeks. The conversation was desultory; George wondered if
the crab bisque was fresh. The prices on the wine list had been
inked out and raised. A bottle of 1973 Chateau Margaux sold
for a hundred and thirty dollars. He realized he might order it;
there was nothing on the menu, no matter how pretentious,
that he could not afford. This recognition troubled him. When
he had first arrived in Saratoga Springs, his apartment cost
less than a hundred and thirty dollars per month; he spent
two months in Barbados, once, on what he would earn from
this trip.

"Let's hear some country music," Sam said. "If you're up
to it. There's the best little band in Knoxville playing at Buddy's
tonight."

"All right."

"If you'd like to hear that band before they get away. . . ."

"Up north, he means," said Ginny. "Or to Nashville."

George paid. They drove to Buddy's, but could not find a
parking space; they parked two streets east. The night air was
wet and warm. It felt, he told the Halls, like New England in
July; girls in T-shirts jostled for position, and boys weaved past,
waving beer. The tables at Buddy's were full. They stood in the
back of the hall and listened to the group; they were playing
"Foggy Mountain Break Down" laboriously. Then the lead
singer said he would imitate Elvis; he performed a hip-grind-
ing version of "You Ain't Nothin' But A Hound Dog." Next he
imitated Tennessee Ernie Ford, and his voice changed timbre
and range: he sang "Sixteen Tons." Then the bass player joined
him, and they harmonized on "Do, Lord, Remember Me," and
then the whole group sang "Carry Me Back To Ol' Virginny."

George, listening, looked at the crowd. There were few

blacks there, and nearly no one of his age; they rocked and clapped and waved their arms with pleasure. He felt none. The noise was jangling, discordant, and the spirituals were offered in the spirit of a barbershop quartet. He asked for coffee, not beer. He excused himself again; this time he reached his wife.

"How is it going?" she asked.

"It's going."

"You don't sound too happy."

"I miss you," he said. "I'm calling from a bluegrass bar with fifty thousand children."

"There's been an accident here," Allyn said. "Betsy Sigurdsen and three of her friends were in a car crash last night."

His first reaction was relief: the twins were safe. He covered his left ear. The band was resting between sets; he blocked out the noise at the bar. Allyn had been notified by the Dean of Students; she apologized for telling him but knew he'd want to know. Four students, carousing at midnight, had wrapped a car around a tree and been hospitalized. The two boys were not badly hurt; they had been wearing seat belts. The driver had a broken arm; his car was wrecked. One girl was in serious condition, with a lung full of blood and both legs broken; she would recover, Allyn said. The prognosis was good. She named those three. "But Betsy is in Albany. They took her there; it's serious. They've been operating all day long."

"What's wrong? Do you know?"

"Her skull was fractured, George. They say the brain pan was exposed; she'll lose an eye at least. The optic nerve was severed."

"Christ."

"She may survive it. She's young. Her vital signs are excellent. I know all this because they're keeping us informed from the Medical Center."

"Christ knows how fast they were going," he said. "Drunk, I imagine. Or stoned."

After some time the conversation shifted. The twins had gone to Sally Rifkin's birthday party and were so tired afterward they fell asleep on the couch; Allyn had been reading Simenon. "Next time you come along," he said. "I've had enough of motel rooms without you."

"My darling carpetbagger," Allyn said. "Just come on back."

Thirty-eight years old, a professor of American history at Skidmore College in Saratoga Springs, George stood in what he liked to think of as an ambiguous relation to undergraduates. He had been a senior when his present freshmen were born. Too old to share his life with them, he nonetheless claimed to prefer their values to his colleagues'. In the sixties he had considered politics; he led the college deputations to Washington, D.C., and felt joyful solidarity when teargassed with his class. At twenty-nine, he married a student. Allyn produced an essay on the *Federalist Papers* that he still considered a model of its kind. Her view of Alexander Hamilton was perhaps a touch overly critical—but otherwise, he wrote, her reading seemed acute. The research had been thorough and the language expressive; the essay was fully first-rate. He hoped she would continue in the field.

She came to his office to contest his opinion of Hamilton, wearing cutoff jeans and a shirt tied up under her breasts. It was October, the height of leaf season; he said he'd just as soon continue this discussion in fresh air. She suggested they go for a drive. She led him to a waterfall she said she wanted him to see, and took his hand approaching the cascade. They found a bower underneath a split-leaf maple flaming in the pines; cows grazed in a meadow beyond a low ridge. Her diaphragm, she told him when he asked, was already in.

They were married the following June. He had a small

inheritance and she too had some money; after Allyn's gradua-
tion, they spent nine months in France. He revised his disserta-
tion, and it became a book. His analysis of Sherman's march
through Georgia, with particular reference to Special Field
Order No. 14, and the present relevance of "Forty acres and a
mule" earned him some attention. His work thereafter on
Tunis G. Campbell and the separatist enclave on the Georgia
Sea Islands brought him renown; when he was offered tenure,
they decided to accept.

"I worry," Allyn sometimes said, "about your students.
Trying to seduce you. Coming on in hallways."

"Don't worry," he would tease her. "It can't happen
here."

"If it happened before it can happen again."

"There's a difference," George said. "Remember?"

"What's the difference?"

"You. And the difference is that I get older, but they stay
the same."

Their daughters were born in 1974, and Saratoga seemed
a safe place to raise them; they purchased a house on the edge
of the campus and he sometimes skied to work. In his sabbatical year the family returned to France; he wrote on the range
of French reaction to the Civil War. Allyn was happy in the
Vaucluse. "I could live here forever," she said. Retentive, he
maintained the Alfa Romeo that she gave him as a wedding
gift; for her birthday two years later he gave her a Jeep
Wagoneer.

From Knoxville he traveled to Shreveport. This confer-
ence was called "Fort Humbug," and George gave the keynote
address. According to local legend, the town had been saved
from assault by pine trees painted black. The fort's com-
mander had ordered them felled and mounted overlooking
the Red River. He had had no ammunition; these trees were
"humbug" guns. The flagship of the Northern fleet, however,

had panicked and retreated; the town remained untouched. The legend was instructive but untrue. George spoke of the varieties of siege, using "Fort Humbug" as an instance of the illusory objective and diversionary assault. This applied to the South as well as the North. In the drama of the Civil War, he said, as with the ancient Greeks—and note the expression "theater of war," notice how historians employ the rhetoric of theater—the consequential actions were taking place offstage.

A lawyer and a doctor and their wives took him to supper that night. He deserved a change of scene, they said; they drove to a nearby lake. Bob Bevis was expansive; he had beer and white wine in the cooler. He was passionate, he said, about good beer—he went to England every summer just to bone up on the dark. He was chief attorney for a local oil consortium and a distribution planning board; big business, Bob said, was about the only place you got serious planning these days. They know those pipelines will be sitting in the ground when there's no oil or gas left to pipe, and they're thinking hard and long about it; they entertain reality scenarios. Those pipelines have got to hold *something,* he said, and that's what we're discussing. "I take my hat off"—he uncapped a beer—"those companies plan in advance."

Horses grazed, and there were squatters' shacks. The woods increased. Then they came to a clearing at lakeside, with houseboats huddled to a dock; an ancient black man hauled jerry cans of gas. "How's things, Brownie?" Bob Bevis asked. The doctor parked his station wagon and locked the four doors. Brownie put down his gas cans and straightened, wiped his hands on his shirt and grinned. His gums were pink; he had no teeth. Bob laughed. He turned to George and said, "You know what I asked him? I asked if there's been any changes 'round here. And he tells me, 'No, not unless *you've* changed.'" They loaded the hampers and cooler and coats on a pink houseboat; the doctor started the motor. Bob laughed again, with proprietary fondness: "'Not unless *you've* changed,'" he said.

There was duckweed in the lake. Cypress trees rose from the water as if it would recede again; ducks scooted ahead. The Spanish moss hung thickly from trees he could not name, and the rising moon was full. The women complained of the cold. Bob distributed drinks. "We could drive to Mermaid Tavern," said his wife, Lucille. "There's a road right up to it. But this is more fun, don't you think? Especially on the way back."

The Mermaid Tavern had electric lanterns on the dock and a stuffed alligator at the entrance door. They drank their wine in paper cups and kept the bottle underneath the table; the tavern had no liquor license. There were murals of mermaids; the kitchen had a carved sign reading, "Davy Jones' Lock-Up!" George ordered boiled shrimp; his bowl was heaped high. The others ordered catfish or combination plates and made him taste their several dishes. "Got to keep your strength up," said Lucille. "That's what I always say."

"Wild nights," said Lynda-Kay across the table. "When the moon gets full like this . . ."

"What's the full moon got to do with it?" her husband asked. "Why wait for the moon?"

George peeled his shrimp and piled the shells on his empty salad plate. He thanked his hosts and, for the moment, meant it: how gracious and hospitable, how open-handed they seemed. The wine was abundant and good. His tongue felt furred. This is a variety of deathlessness, he said, a truce with time. He proposed a toast to Master Death and how they had outwitted him this night, how paper cups are goblets when newfound friends agree. His hosts agreed. They said, "Your health," and drank, but his speech had been discordant. Death and immortality were not proper topics to raise.

Allyn and the twins collected him on Sunday. He brought back Confederate flags, breakfast grits and a miniature bale of cotton. Patty and Sarah told him their news, how they played musical chairs and blindman's buff and could see right through the blindfold at Sally Rifkin's party, and how much they missed him every night. He drove. Allyn took his hand and pressed it to the inside of her knee.

That night he called the Sigurdsens; they said he would be welcome whenever he could come. Betsy was still in danger, and blind in her right eye—but miracle of miracles, her mother said over the phone, there seemed to be no damage to the brain. The doctors had been wonderful; they had had to throw away six pieces of the skull. "No one seems to understand," her mother said, "how Betsy made it through that operation. Or the crash. Of course we've prayed and prayed, and now we have to keep our fingers crossed."

He went south the following Friday, after his ten o'clock class. The day was overcast but warm; he drove with the Alfa's top down. It was Indian summer, the end of October, and he packed jogging clothes in the trunk. On the way back, he told Allyn, he'd stop off somewhere for a quick run. "I can taste it already," he said. "The smell of that hospital room. The stink of machinery"—he clucked his tongue—"you know how I hate hospitals."

"Drive carefully," she said. "Send Betsy all our love."

He kissed her. "Yes. When's their ballet lesson over— five? I'll be back before that. Soon."

The car responded well. They had purchased it in Milano and shipped it home from Marseilles; he had had it rust-proofed and repainted. On the Northway and in Albany the Alfa drew attention; he closed and locked it in the hospital parking lot. At the entrance he bought roses from a woman in a wheelchair. "Bless you and yours," she said.

Betsy Sigurdsen was in room 752. "Relatives only," they said at the desk.

"I'm her professor," George said. "Her parents asked me to come."

He walked down the hall, knocked and hesitated. "Her mother's inside," said a nurse. She lay on the bed, white hospital sheet at her hips, head shaved, her eyes like a raccoon's. There were black crescents under them, then a white arc of flesh. "Hel*lo*," she said.

"Hello." His throat was dry; he cleared it. "How are you, Betsy?"

"Tip-top," she said. "Look who's here." She shrugged, then winced at the gesture and put out her hand. He showed her the flowers and bent down to kiss her; she shrank at the touch of his lips. "Yow," Betsy said. "Don't mind me. It's just I hurt all over."

She rearranged her shift. The pattern on her skull seemed familiar, and he shut his eyes and saw a piece of cloth with stitches while Allyn taught the twins. Her sewing machine was black; the cloth would be cross-hatched and stippled with thread. He turned to Betsy's mother and said, "Mrs. Sigurdsen?"

"Yes. We've heard *so* much about you."

"Some of it good, I hope."

"Oh, all of it. Those flowers. I'd best get a vase for them. Water."

"Don't bother. They can wait."

"I'll do it now. I know just where the vases are. I'll be right back."

She hurried out; there were flowers all over the room.

"How are you really?" George asked.

"She's scared of you." Betsy lifted her arm. "She's been wonderful, though. I hurt all over."

"Do you want to talk about it?"

"No. It wasn't Bill's fault. He wasn't drunk. We'd all been studying and stayed up late and had just one beer maybe, and he fell asleep at the wheel."

"You don't have to protect him."

"I know. Three beers, maybe."

"What matters is you made it. You're alive."

"My nose is my best feature, don't you think? And that hasn't been broken. And I haven't eaten so I'll lose a lot of weight." She put her hand up to her head. "Do I look awful?"

"No."

"I do. You never saw my ears before."

"You look beautiful," he said. And it was true, absurdly, as she lay before him, her skull that had been masked by hair now naked, egg-shaped, the whole of her face jarred loose from its bone-struts and smashed. The left side of her head seemed lower than the right; symmetry had gone. She had been rearranged. She worked an eyepatch into place over the blind right eye. "You mean that?" Betsy asked.

Her mother returned. "There"—she placed the roses on the windowsill—"we'll give them the place of honor. Long-stemmed roses, Betsy—aren't we fortunate?"

"My father left. I *wish* you could have met him," said the girl.

"He'll be back," said Mrs. Sigurdsen. "We've never been to Albany before."

Then they conversed about the airplane trip from Raleigh-Durham through Atlanta to Albany and the relative merits of Atlanta and O'Hare. The Sigurdsens had moved to Chapel Hill. Mrs. Sigurdsen said everybody at the hospital was wonderful; you couldn't beat this hospital for kindness, the Women's Auxiliary Club had an apartment for visiting parents, and she'd brought her needlepoint and was snug as a bug in a rug. Of course, she hoped that they'd be home by Thanksgiving, but there's so much to be thankful for she wouldn't mind it in the slightest if they had to stay till Christmas and eat their turkey dinner sitting by this bed. You get used to things, she said, there's no use complaining, if you've got to make do you make do. You get out of the woods if you wait.

A nurse arrived with pills. "Now swallow these, dearie," she said.

Betsy made a face at him; he studied the curtainless window. His roses seemed crimson, and wax. The problem is, said Mrs. Sigurdsen, there's all this spinal fluid coming from her nose; if it doesn't stop leaking they'll operate again. He told Betsy not to worry about course work or credit or reading; she said she worried, anyhow. He asked if there were messages she'd like to send, or people she would like to see, and she said, "No. Just you again. You've been so kind. And I know how terrifically busy you must be. He's the busiest teacher on campus, Mom, he's so sought after. You wouldn't believe it."

"I believe it, dear. From everything I've heard."

George sat at the bed's edge. He felt prized beyond his value, and hot in his tweed coat.

"You have two lovely daughters, Betsy says. How old would they be?"

"Six," George told her. "They're twins."

"And your wife's name?"

"Allyn." He made his old joke. "She's got a man's first name, so she married a man with a woman's name last."

Mrs. Sigurdsen smiled. "Allyn Allison. She must be beautiful."

"She is, Mom," Betsy said.

He recited Sarah's poem. That morning, eating her soft-boiled egg and English muffin, mouth full, she had announced, "I wrote a poem, Daddy. Want to hear it?" He told her to finish her muffin and then he would listen. She swallowed and said:

> Day chases morning,
> Evening chases day;
> Night chases evening,
> And all fades away.

"How wonderful!" said Mrs. Sigurdsen.

"I *told* you," Betsy said. "Didn't I tell you? Too much." She settled back, breasts bobbing, as if the achievement were hers. She smiled at him, raising her legs. The swelling underneath her eyes increased at this angle; he stood.

"I ought to be going. The nurse said not to tire you."

"You only just got here."

"I'll be back."

"How's the Dred Scott decision?" she wanted to know. "Is that what you're doing in class?"

"It's fine. Yes. You'll be released in no time and come to the house for a drink."

"Oh, George," she wailed, "I'm not allowed to. The doctors won't let me. Nothing to drink. Or smoke. Or anything."

He kissed her hand. "Be patient. See you soon."

"A patient patient, that's our girl." Mrs. Sigurdsen ushered him out. In the corridor she said, "She wouldn't want me saying this, but your visit has made Betsy's day. Thank you so much for the flowers."

"Take care," George said. "Be well."

"I hope you never know, Professor—I hope you never have to feel what we're feeling today. Those beautiful daughters of yours, those marvelous bright children . . ." She took his sleeve, detaining him. The hall seemed improbably dark. "I hope by the time they grow up, when they are Betsy's age, I pray there's no more cars in America."

"It wasn't her fault," he offered.

"No. It never is. It's always someone else's fault, it's always some drunken lunatic coming at you in the wrong lane. Or falling asleep at the wheel. It's always somebody else's problem when your life gets wrecked."

"I'm sorry."

"Yes. I have to have someone to talk to. That passage in the Bible, do you know it, 'Absalom'?" She closed her eyes; her voice changed register. "It's just exactly how I feel, it's just what I keep saying: 'Oh Absalom my son. Would to God I had died for you. Would to God I had died for you, my son . . .'"

He kissed her cheek. When he turned at the elevator and looked back, she was still standing there, her eyes squeezed shut like fists.

Returning, he took secondary roads. He drove past barge canals and bridges, past feed corn being cut and the fair ground standing empty now, its placards proclaiming last month's county fair. He had been more stirred by such bruised nakedness than he could reveal. Betsy Sigurdsen had been his student for three years. She was pretty enough, and pert, full of an avid anxiousness to learn, with an appetite for facts. Her ankles were thick, shoulders broad. While others in his seminar would shake their heads and frown at documents or use his carefully amassed files of microfilm only at term-paper time, Betsy would swallow whole volumes of data and spew forth dates as if they signified: she *saw* the decline in Sea Island long-staple cotton in 1856, she would say, like the shirt off a gentleman's back.

She often stopped him in the halls and asked for an appointment; she came to office hours every week. So he grew familiar with her history, the rigor of her background and her skill at horseback riding, the decision to come north from Chapel Hill; she was the only student in her high school class, she told him, who studied in New York State. Her elder sister had left home and worked for American Airlines; she traveled all around the world and sent back postcards always ending, "Wish you could be here!" She had boyfriends and she blushed but talked about them, anyhow: the way she could outlast them if they took on a bottle, or tennis, how Robert or Philip could dance. He knew about her trouble with her jaw, the way it would lock open in what she called intimate acts.

He knew her aspirations too: she dreamed of graduate school. He himself had gone to Brown and promised a recommendation; he saw no reason why she shouldn't persevere. Her particular cluster of aptitudes, George said, could well make a historian; she had been preparing for the Graduate Record Exams.

The sky was gray. He listened to the weather forecast, after the three o'clock news. He loosened his tie and, at a traffic light, pulled off his shoes. What troubled him was how his visit had eradicated distance, as if their teacher-student stance had been a sham for years. She had displayed herself as if to a suitor, not a friend. Her ankles had been hidden in the blanket-tangle underneath his hand. He thought of her with love.

George shook his head. He consulted his watch; he had time for a run. He slowed and made a detour to the right. It was farm country here, hilly, and he concentrated on the drive: unpainted barns and silos and corncribs and a stock pond in the rain. The road had been recently tarred. He passed a sign saying "Windy Hill Farm. Maple Syrup. Eggs." and remembered having been this way before: The town of Schuylerville lay beneath and if he went due east he'd come to the river. He mapped out his run.

She'd said, "Or smoke. Or anything," and shifted in the sheets as if to a rhythm they shared. Death had embraced her one week before, and now she understood more of mortality than he. He double-clutched, advancing into fourth.

Directions: he had lived his life by them. What signs he read he followed; what turns he made he made with adequate warning and judiciously. He had been faithful to his wife, despite her half-serious fears; his career was going well. And he adored his daughters; had Mrs. Sigurdsen asked to see their photographs he would gladly have pulled out his wallet. He had taken the girls to Woolworth's for a set of pictures. The visiting photographer had placed them on a table, instructing them to hold hands and how to smile and when to smile and how to hold their positions. He changed the backdrop poster several times. They sat first before a sylvan scene, then by a snowy mountain, then in front of a picket fence. The Allisons would get a complimentary eight-by-ten, he said; they could select the poses they preferred.

George found the session bizarre. The photographer insisted on making the twins laugh. He put a beanbag Snoopy on his head, then let it fall; he tried to eat a handkerchief, saying, "Whoopsiedoodle"; he asked them to call him "Potatohead" or "Cabbagemouth." They did not dare, and he urged them. "Call me Cabbagemouth," he said. "I promise, I don't mind." So, tentative, politely, they pronounced "Potatohead" and "Cabbagemouth."

"Louder," he said. "I didn't quite hear."

"*Pota*tohead," said Sarah. "Cabbagemouth," said Patty.

"*What* did you call me?" the photographer roared. The twins giggled, and he pressed the buttons for the flash.

So George possessed wallet-size photos of the girls embracing before a picket fence. He hoped that they might stay that way: intimate yet separable. He thought of taking Betsy in, of asking her to spend her convalescence in their house. He saw a car nose out beneath him on a dirt road to his right. He braked and swerved and honked his horn, but the car continued. It blocked the intersection, then it stopped. He screamed. In the instant of collision, George saw several things: the raw, shocked face of the boy behind the wheel, the way the others in the car—a brown Chevy with a red rear fender—had waved the driver forward till he froze in the T. With three feet more he might have made it, but there was no chance, no choice; George headed for the right rear fender, then the ditch. The shock of impact swung him back; he hit again, this time less solidly, with his left rear panel on the Chevy's driver's door. There was much broken glass. His radiator steamed. The engine continued to run; he switched it off. He felt for injuries, felt none. "You've done it; now you've really gone and done it," he said aloud, several times.

The boy in the other car rolled down his window. "Are you all right?" he asked. His voice was high-pitched.

"I think so. You?"

The boy nodded. George counted slowly, carefully: there were five others in the car. "Is anybody hurt?" he asked.

"No."

There was blood on his cheek from a small shard of glass, and his stomach ached where the seat belt cinched him; he released the belt. Methodically, moving with a thoroughness that imitated calm, George put on his shoes and tightened his tie and stepped out. His elegant indulgence had crumpled in the crash. There was chrome and glass and rubber all around him, and a stream of water. He bent and sniffed for gas. The cars stood alongside each other companionably, like animals—hissing, snuffling, snout to tail.

"You might have waited."

"I know," the boy said. "They told me to try it. They *told* me."

"This your car?"

"My dad's. He'll have a shit fit." The boy was close to tears, was just past driving age and in the kind of trouble he would have sworn that morning to avoid.

The Alfa did not move. George wrenched the wheel back from the fender that braked it. He peered into the Chevrolet and saw three girls, three boys, a six-pack. "Bury that beer," he advised.

"*I* wasn't drinking."

"The sheriff's going to ask you that . . ."

"I could have made it," the boy said. "If only I'd stepped on the gas."

"You could have done a lot of things. You could have stayed at the stop sign, for instance. Just stopped there, like it says. You could have tried reverse. You could have accelerated straight across the road and up that driveway, maybe. The only thing you couldn't do was what you did do, friend, take the whole road. . . ." He straightened, exhaling. "I hope you're insured."

"Yes."

"Because this car's expensive. They don't make them anymore." He had the odd sensation, standing while the children sat, that he was in some lecture hall. There was a farm to his left. A woman advanced with a broom in her hand. "It's a bad corner," she said, commencing to sweep off the glass.

"We ought to make some calls," said George. "Would you have a phone in the house?"

She nodded, pointed to the kitchen door, and he and the boy walked in. Bob Folsom and he exchanged names. Then George produced his driver's license, registration and insurance card, and the boy did likewise and they copied numbers; they called the state police and a local wrecker, and Bob called his parents and they said they'd come to get him. George called Allyn last.

"Hello?"

"Hello. Not to worry," he said. He attempted to steady his voice.

"What's wrong?"

"I'm all right. Nothing's wrong."

"George, what's the matter? Where are you?"

"On Windy Hill Road," he said. "At some no-name intersection on the way to Victory Mills. Off of Johnson Hill. Near Schuylerville, you know. Route Twenty-nine. The bitch of it is that if I'd been driving at something like speed I'd have been long past that T."

"What T? What are you talking about?"

"I had an accident," he said. "I'm all right, though. I am. Nobody's hurt. The car's a wreck."

"Darling . . ."

"Maybe we can fix it. Maybe there's replacement parts. It wasn't my fault, Allyn. I haven't been so law-abiding in that car for *years*."

"The car doesn't matter," she said. "I'm coming to get you."

"Yes. Have someone pick up the kids, will you, from ballet? Ask Eloise. I wouldn't want them to see this."

"No."

"You know the directions?"

"I do."

The taste of tin was in his mouth; he rubbed his hands for heat. He had a headache; his neck hurt. Outside, the state police had arrived and were directing traffic, taking measurements of tire marks and consulting with the riders in the Chevy. He approached.

"That your car?" the sheriff asked.

"It is."

"Afternoon, Professor," someone said. He turned. "A shame," said Billy Peck. "About this car."

"Yes. No one's hurt, though. That's what counts."

"They'll ticket him," Billy confided. "For failure to stop at a stop sign. I happened to be passing through."

"Yes."

"You got some scratches, Professor. I could call the ambulance."

"No. Thank you. My wife's on the way."

"Go check in at the hospital," Billy said. "The emergency room—takes ten minutes. I got a radio, I'll let them know you're coming. Just have them look you over, just in case." He lowered his voice, respectful. "It's better for insurance claims. "If you plan to file them. . . ."

"I was going jogging," George explained. "You won't believe it, but I've just come from the hospital. Not this one, not the one in Saratoga. The Medical Center. I was down in Albany. I was visiting . . ." His voice trailed off. They were not listening, had turned to greet the wrecker. Rain was falling steadily, but to the west sun shone. Bob Folsom's father had appeared and was shouting at his son. They waved their arms like pinwheels; Mrs. Folsom intervened. "The main thing is nobody's hurt," she said. "Let's thank our lucky stars."

Crows gleaned in the corn stubble, and there were penned turkeys and hogs. The wrecker whistled, studying the Alfa. "A collector's item, this one is. Knocked the Chevy clean off its frame. You wouldn't think it, but *that* baby's totaled." He jerked his head over his shoulder. "Now this one here, we'll see."

George walked in circles, waiting. The farmer's wife invited him to have some coffee if he wanted, and he thanked her but refused. She said he could wait in the kitchen; he told her he needed the air. He gave his deposition. They treated him with courtesy, with the attentive deference due to rank and age. He watched the sports car being hooked up, hauled away. He remembered, as the tow truck lumbered past, that his jogging gear was in the trunk; he signaled the wrecker to stop and extracted the brown paper bag. The sheriff watched him distantly. He pulled his sweatshirt from the bag so the man would not suspect a bottle and, holding it, walked down the road in order to intercept Allyn. A dog appeared and menaced him. She would be driving south.

SOME IN THEIR BODY'S FORCE

I n the spring of his junior year at college, Peter Danto fell, as he put it, in lust. It was 1962, and he had turned nineteen; he was trying on his attitudes like clothes. That spring he wanted a life in the theater. He played supporting roles in *Major Barbara* and *Othello* and Jean-Paul Sartre's *The Flies*. In this last play he portrayed King Aegisthus—jaded, motivated not so much by desire as reason.

Clytemnestra's name was Inger; she was attending Radcliffe for a year. He had heard rumors about her. She had that glacial blond beauty supposed to be characteristic of Swedes, and she was rich. Her father was variously reported as a prince, a chancellor of the university, the designer of Volvos and a shipping magnate. She was the Ping-Pong champion of

Europe, the youngest of seven sisters. She carried a gun in her
purse, it was whispered, and when she went home she was
slated to marry a duke.

The director said he wanted her for Clytemnestra because of her accent. The director was of the opinion that the
cast should know why they had been chosen; he went
around the table, discussing attributes. According to his, the
director's, opinion, the queen should be an alien presence
in Argos. It was a play about pretension and unpretentious-
ness; Inger had the latter quality, he said. The director
wanted *The Flies* to be about estrangement, and he repeated
this often.

Her face was round and soft, her feet were bare. She was
high-breasted and slim-hipped; she wore a green striped tank
top and white skirt. Her laugh came easily. They read through
their parts without stopping, and Peter focused—in the intervals when Aegisthus was silent—on Inger's legs: the way they
tapered to her ankles, the muscularity, the hint of less firm
flesh above the knee. He invited her for coffee; she said yes.

There was a coffee shop nearby called Casablanca; photographs of Bogart, Ingrid Bergman and Sidney Greenstreet
lined the bar. Boccherini emerged from the walls. Peter and
Inger selected a table in a green bower of plants. He discoursed on the Oresteia, its relevance to the Vichy government
and Nazi-occupied France. Sartre's text belonged, he said, to
the literature of resistance: it was an inquiry into power, a par-
able of usage and abuse.

They ordered *cappuccino*. She watched, wide-eyed. He
would remember the components of that instant: lamplight,
music, the Danish pastry, the speculative intensity with which
they disagreed. When she shook her head for emphasis, her
yellow hair cascaded. Reaching for the sugar, he grazed her

hand with his hand. *"Du schwarzer Zigeuner,"* she said.
"What does that mean?"
"You dark gypsy. *'Ach,'"*—she hummed a phrase—*"'du schwarzer Zigeuner.'"*
"Tell me about Uppsala."
"There's little to tell," Inger said. "We have a house like you'd imagine: many windows with flowerpots. Fir trees by the balcony."
"Do you miss it?"
"A little."
"Right now?"
"My father's very serious," she said. "You, Peter, are you serious?"
"I'm a bad actor," he said.
She disconcerted him by taking this at face value; he had assumed she'd smile. "Then why do you do it?" she asked.
He drank. "I don't know, really."
"For fun," said Inger. "To show you're not my father."
She smiled. Her front teeth were uneven. They talked about their roles. Peter said that killing Agamemnon had been, in Clytemnestra's case, not so much a matter of sexual passion or envy as an *acte gratuit.* It all hinged, he maintained, on whether Agamemnon had slept with Clytemnestra before his ritual cleansing in the bath. If she killed him after sex, there might indeed have been a passionate revulsion. But if she killed her husband while he washed, the knife thrust was dispassionate, a mating dance enacted for the audience. The text suggested this was so: Agamemnon's feet were smelly, his hair unclean. So he was prinking up for purity—getting ready, making certain not to mess the carpets. Offstage, Cassandra was being gang-banged by the palace guard.
Inger swallowed. Foam from the *cappuccino* flecked her upper lip. He was making it all up, of course, aroused by her attention. He felt reckless and inventive; he asked about

her sisters and she told him she had none. When they parted for the evening, she pressed against him briefly—and they agreed to meet again after rehearsal that week.

Peter lived in Adams House. His room had bay windows that gave on a courtyard, a sleeping alcove and a bathroom lined with tile. There was what once had been a functioning fireplace; the walls were wood-paneled. He could pretend to independence once inside the door, but the foyer of his entry was a trial. She printed her name in block letters on the sign-in sheet. Laundry was being delivered on the second floor. Inside, he kissed her several times. Inger was, suddenly, shy. He fumbled with her buttons while she sat on the bed.

"Be careful," Inger said.

Her body was thin, her breasts small. She said, "I want some music," and he played *Leon Bibb Sings Love Songs* on his new stereo set. At "The Water Is Wide" he took off his shoes and, during "Down In The Valley," he removed his shirt. He was self-conscious about this, since he had many pimples on his back. When she closed her eyes, he closed his also, in gratitude. They kissed again and, some seconds later, he opened his eyes to find her watching him. They smiled. When he pulled back her hair, her face had a baby's smooth roundness, and the small hairs at her neck were white. He said, "I want to be with you," and tugged off her skirt. He took off his pants and lay down.

Leon Bibb completed "Dance To Your Daddy" and began again. His voice was high. Peter penetrated Inger; she was unresistant. She was not helpful, however, and seemed to be in pain. He asked her if she was worried, and she shook her head; he asked her, was it safe for him to be inside her, and she said she took the Pill. He asked her, was she happy being on his casting couch, and she tried to smile. He pretended expertise.

When they finished, she was bleeding. She said, "I

thought I was no virgin," and covered herself with the sheets. He assured her that she could be bleeding because he touched some part that had not previously been reached. She said, "You think so, Peter?" and he said he hoped so, yes. He felt triumphal, huge. He produced a towel and she said, "I want to shower."

"I'll join you," Peter said.

In the shower she sang to him, softly. Her high spirits had returned. She soaped him, and they pressed up against each other, and he said Aegisthus had a better time than Agamemnon in his bath. "It'll be better next time," he said.

"What will?"

"The sex. It's always an improvement the second time."

This was not a statement he could verify. Inger placed the soap back in the soap dish, rinsed herself off and stepped out of the stall. By the time he too emerged, she was dry and collecting her clothes.

"Is something wrong?" he asked.

"No."

"What is it?"

"'It'll be better the next time,'" she said.

"I'm sorry."

"You make me feel foolish."

"No."

"Could you *please* turn off that record?" Inger asked.

He could not bring himself to say the line was borrowed, that he'd read it in a book. "We have to get to rehearsal," he said.

"Yes."

"Are you hungry?"

She shook her head.

"Will I see you again?"

"At rehearsal," she said.

His daughter went to school in Arizona. They had argued

lengthily as to whether she should go that far, whether she was old enough or really had to leave. The local school system, said Judy, was so destructive they had no choice; peer pressure to fail was too great. She had been learning nothing but the names of drugs and cars. "One more year like this," said Judy, "and our little darling will have her own little darlings. We've got to get her out."

So they sent her to a boarding school in the suburbs of Tucson. The admissions officer admired Lucinda. "She's one tough cookie, isn't she?" he asked. Peter felt forced to agree. She was thick-tongued and torpid, who had been his quicksilver child. She fell in love, that first semester, with a horse named Bill. She wrote detailed descriptions, with photography enclosed, of Bill at rest and eating, of Bill in his stall or by the river, in the mountains, with the ribbons that she won for riding him in novice class.

By spring she was no novice, and Peter purchased a thousand-dollar saddle. He bought her boots and a coat and cap and tack; he sent her books on *dressage*. Judy said he was being extravagant, doting from a distance, and Peter agreed. But he preferred to picture her in stalls than on the back seats of cars; he'd rather that she mucked about with horses than with punks. Lucinda called on his birthday and said, "Bill loves you too."

"We haven't met," said Peter.

"No. But you should see him, Daddy. With that saddle."

"Yes."

"He's got you to thank. So we both wish you happy birthday."

"Thank you, darling."

"I'm going to buy him," she said. "Right now he belongs to the whole school."

"I'm on the upstairs phone," said Judy. "Buy *who*?"

"With the money Nanno left me. I can do what I want with it, right?"

He shifted the receiver. "I'm not sure Nanno meant it that way."

"Bill's mine," she said. "He knows it too. He just despises it if any other girl gets on. That Missy Tief, for instance."

"It's your father's birthday," Judy said. "Not yours. We'll discuss this later."

"Happy birthday, Daddy."

"Yes."

"I'll see you in three weeks."

"We miss you," Peter said.

He had broken his ankle; he walked with a cane. He had fallen down the office stairs. Since he was vice-president of an insurance agency, this called forth humor from friends. "How about your coverage?" they asked. "Does it cover your own office? What's the policy on sliding down a banister instead?"

The stairs were wide and smooth, no obstacle. He traveled them ten times a day. Later he would ask himself what had been the distraction, what whiff of springtime in the air or birdsong or engine caused him to fall. He landed unevenly; his right ankle buckled and he heard a single, popping sound. He lay there, then built himself back to his feet. He could not put weight on the foot. He stood, leaning against the wall of the building, feeling the brick, balancing, waiting for what seemed a rainstorm to subside. There was no rainstorm, but there was a roaring in his ears, and the air went cold. He sat. His head dropped to his knees. He spent some time deciding if his head dropped to his knees involuntarily or whether he had lowered it on purpose. Blood coursed through his head. It felt palpable, a liquid he could see with his eyes closed.

The village of Sandgate, their home, celebrated Memorial Day. Peter took his son to the parade. Sam was nine, excited. They had an invitation to Mrs. Welling's porch. They walked together from West Street to Main Street, slowly. "Do you miss your sister?" Peter asked.

Sam shrugged.

"Having someone to go to the pool with?"

"No."

"Why not?"

"She never takes me."

"This summer she will," Peter promised. "And she'll teach you tennis too."

"I bet."

"She plans to," Peter said.

"Do you think you'll play tennis again?"

His cane was ebony, with a steel tip, and intricately carved. He flourished it. "Of course."

"I want *you* to teach me," said Sam.

"I'll come along. I'll be coach."

"She'll probably go horseback riding."

"Well, I want to see her."

"I don't."

Larry Welling, Jr., waited on the porch. Larry was fifty, a bachelor. "How's the leg?"

"It's mending," Peter said. He settled himself on a chaise longue. "They've cut me out of the cast."

Larry was a large man, blockish, fond of fishing; his hair was white. Sandgate perched on the Cold River, along the Mohawk Trail.

Mrs. Welling appeared. "You handsome man," she said. "You sit right there."

He put a hand on Sam's neck. "The boys' day out," he said. "We're giving Judy a rest."

"Good morning," Mrs. Welling said to Sam. She poured lemonade. "Could I interest you in this?"

"Say 'thank you,'" Peter said.

"Thank you."

She was seventy-seven years old, she told anyone who

asked, and just as much inclined to dance as way back when; if
you asked her to go waltzing she'd be happy to accept.

Sarah Beame closed the screen door. The porch required
paint. "How's Judy?"

"She's on a diet."

"Oh? Which one?"

"The Scarsdale one," said Sam. He perched himself on
Peter's chair. "The one where the doctor got killed."

The adults laughed. Volunteer firemen assembled. The
bowling team captain was Sam's teacher, and he noticed Sam
and waved. It had rained that morning, and the lawns were
wet. The sidewalk glistened, and Main Street was washed,
expectant.

Mrs. Welling offered pie. "I'll cut a piece for Judy too. You
take it back to her."

"Lemon meringue," Peter said. "She'd shoot me."

Fred Peaslee walked up the steps. He stretched, then took
a seat. "How'd you do last night?" asked Larry.

"Well, hello," Fred said. "Everybody."

"There was birds last night," said Larry. The sun angled
into the porch.

Fred drew his index finger sharply past his throat.
"Birds," he said. "I never did like to bet birds."

"Dogs, though. Now that's another thing."

"Not me. I got no stomach for it." Fred sighed. "I take a
lady to the track, and if they're racing dogs, why then I'll sit on
my hands."

Mrs. Welling turned to Sam. "You eat this piece we saved
for your mother, okay? Or have some gingersnaps."

Sam took two. A Labrador barked in its sleep. A girl
walked by in white thong sandals; the light outlined her legs.
Sam went, "Oompah, oompapah" and leaned out over the rail.
Peter felt a spasm of excitement, a sudden lifting. The girl
smiled—at him, possibly, or at the tableau on the porch. They

were at home here; this was home; he accepted coffee in dead
Mr. Welling's own cup.

Peter and Inger went walking together one Thursday; it
was a fine spring day. They walked through Cambridge streets
and then the Mt. Auburn cemetery; there were fresh flowers
everywhere, and many people visiting. They looked at marble
griffins and studied the inscriptions on the more imposing
crypts. Inger was familiar with the creed of Christian Scientists.
Mary Baker Eddy was supposedly not dead, she said, but just
asleep; a telephone was supposed to be kept near the grave.
When Mary Baker Eddy woke up and wanted something, the
only thing she had to do was make her wishes known.

They found themselves in streets he did not recognize,
with family grocery stores and plumbing shops and bars. They
continued. The sun was hot. He was wearing old, torn clothes,
and his hair was long; the crowd looked at him with disdain.
Men stared at Inger openly, and some of them whistled and
snickered. He heard a drumroll down the street, the sound of
trumpets and then a band playing.

"Where are we?" Inger asked.

"Watertown, I think."

"So many people here," she said. "For lunch."

Men sold balloons and ice cream; there were crepe-paper
garlands on the lampposts. Men waved flags. "I just remembered," Peter said. "It's Memorial Day."

The sound increased. There were floats and police cars
and, in the nearing distance, the sound of piccolos. She
clapped her hands delightedly. "Let's watch."

They took positions by a fire hydrant. Policemen on
motorcycles rolled past. The queen of the parade was draped
in red, white and blue. Her float was flower-strewn. She
twirled a baton in her left hand and blew kisses with her right;
she switched hands as she drove by Peter and Inger and, for a
moment, lost the beat. There were horses and firemen and

men from the Rotary Club walking in business suits; there were Boy Scouts in uniform, and Little Leaguers with the legend of their sponsors on their backs. Men held banners and wore sashes reading "United Way."

"Do you want a hot dog?" Peter asked.

"A what?"

"A frankfurter," he said. "A little sausage in a bun."

She laughed. "I know what a hot dog is, silly. I didn't hear your question."

"Well, do you want one?"

"Yes."

He tried to attract the vendor's attention but failed. The man pushed on, clanging his bell. Then the sky went dark. It was without significance, a single shadow, yet the scene in front of Peter darkened in aspect also. Something triggered a store-front alarm. Inger wore a white dress that buttoned to the waist, with mother-of-pearl buttons and a ruff of eyelet lace. He was with a foreign woman while the Veterans of Foreign Wars paraded down Main Street. He himself was alien, a make-believe gypsy whose pockets were full. He took Inger by the elbow and stepped back.

"How was it?" Judy asked them.

"Fine."

"Did you enjoy yourself?" She took Sam's coat.

"Mm-mn. I'm hungry."

"Didn't Daddy get you anything?"

"Just pie."

"And gingersnaps," said Peter. "And lemonade. Potato chips."

"I'm *still* hungry."

"Yogurt," Judy said. "That's what we're having for lunch."

"With honey and raisins?"

"With raisins," she said.

Judy was polishing silver. She did this when dieting in

order to keep out of the kitchen and still keep her hand in, she said. Today she was so hungry she could eat the knife.

"'I eat my peas with honey,'" Peter said. "'I've done so all my life. It might taste kind of funny, but it keeps them on the knife.'"

"Did you thank Mrs. Welling?" she asked.

"We did."

"And how was the parade?"

"Fine."

"Not long enough," said Peter.

Judy turned back to the spoons. She had demitasse spoons and soup spoons and teaspoons and serving spoons on the table in the dining alcove; she had completed the forks.

"Can we go swimming?" Sam asked.

"Not now."

"But Tony's going swimming."

"I can't take you," Peter said. "And your mother's busy."

"How's the leg?" she asked him.

"All right. I sat and watched things, mostly."

Tony Neff appeared. They can't go to the pool, his parents have decided, but could they go in the woods? Peter cored an apple, offered a portion to each of the boys—giving his son, scrupulously, the smaller piece—and said yes. They ran to their fort in the woods. Peter watched them as they cartwheeled down the slope: motion unrestricted. He moved to where his wife was sitting, leaned down and kissed her hair. "How was your morning?"

Judy set the rag and polish on a serving tray. "I have a headache," she said.

"Maybe it's the silver polish."

"No. This diet."

"You look terrific," he said.

"Five more pounds. Five more and I'll weigh what I weighed when we married."

"Five *less* pounds."

"You know what I'm saying."

"I love you."

"Yes."

He lowered himself to a chair. "Let's take a trip."

"Where?"

"Anywhere," he said. "Sweden, maybe. Or Norway. I've never seen a fjord."

His failure to have seen a fjord seemed, for an instant, serious. Peter closed his eyes. Mrs. Welling had been affable, solicitous. She walked them to the intersection at the bank.

The family went to Prince Island in July. They rented a house on the north shore; theirs was a private beach. Judy had spent summers on the island in her childhood, and she said the place was magic still, a panacea for each ailment of the soul. She meant that sentiment, she said, although it might sound overwrought. They have proven lately that sunshine makes a person cheerful, whereas clinical depression can be induced by the dark.

Who's proved that? Peter asked, and she said psychologists. Sociologists, he said, or physiologists maybe, but it sounded wishful to him—the kind of attitude induced by skillful advertising, a tourist bureau somewhere that needed to drum up new trade. Well, anyway, she said, this island is my magic place, it's everything *I* need. It's long days lazing on the beach, and fish, and gin and tonics on the porch at sunset, a chance to play Scrabble and dream.

Helicopters buzzed the coast. Peter listened to the radio. He ate and swam without urgency. Men stood by the wharf, surfcasting. They had waders on, or bathing suits; they had Styrofoam coolers, and beer. Where fish broke the water, or birds gathered, or where there was a sudden darkness, men cast; they stood for hours, smoking, catching nothing he could see. Sometimes a rod would stiffen and bend; there would be a flurry of adjustments, a palpable attention. Then the line would part or the rod go slack, the fisherman would bring in a piece of dripping wool or wood.

Peter watched. He himself was thick-fingered; he had no desire to fish. But something in the manner of the men at the tide line compelled him; they had an equilibrium and a purpose he lacked. They were hunting something and it did not matter if they caught it, yet it mattered how they caught it and how they passed the time. They focused on procedure with the passion of initiates. He lay and drank and dozed. He was healing, he assured himself; he had been more tired than he knew.

On Saturday evening there was a dance at the Grange. Lucinda did not want to go; she was grossed out by square dancing, she said. It was definitely not copacetic, all those boys with cowboy hats and gum. So Judy drove Sam to the hall and Peter returned to collect him. A woman approached his parked car.

"Peter Danto?"

He recognized her vaguely. "Yes?"

"I'm Janice Esterman. You knew me as Saxe. Janice Saxe."

"Of course." He opened the car door, embarrassed.

"You haven't changed," she said. He stood. She offered him her hand.

"It's lovely to see you."

"I mean it. You look just the same."

"Our eyes get older," he pronounced, "along with the object perceived."

She smiled. Her breasts were fuller than he remembered, her ankles more substantial. She wore expensive, casual clothes: white pants with a drawstring, a silk shirt. Her sandals were gold, her skin dark. They made conversation about what he was doing here, about coincidence and how long it had been since they last met.

"Are you married?" she asked.

"Yes. With two children."

"Your first wife?"

He nodded. "And you?"

"Congratulations," Janice said. "That's some kind of record, I think. I'm in the process myself."

"Of marriage?"

"Divorce. We've been divorcing since we got married. Sometimes it seems like"—she laughed—"since *before* we got married. But this time there's lawyers involved."

The square dance was over. Children jostled out of the Grange, some with their arms still crossed or do-si-do-ing with their partners. Doors slammed. Mothers started their car radios and turned on their lights. "Are these two yours?" he asked.

"Lydia. Bill. Meet Peter Danto."

"I knew your mother long ago." He coughed, then cleared his throat. "It's nice to meet her children."

Sam appeared. He came to Peter shyly. They repeated introductions, and Lydia said, "We met inside. At the Virginia Reel."

Janice was scanning the crowd; she gave him her profile. He watched. The memory of sex, he thought, can be as powerful as its expectation; their one previous encounter compelled him now again. He remembered it in detail and with clarity. They had gone to the movies together in August in Manhattan; it was a wet night. She wore dungarees and a wool shirt, and the shapelessness of her apparel made her seem all the more shapely by contrast. He invited her back for a drink. When she accepted he had known she would accept him also; she put her arm around his waist as they waited for the light.

"I have to go now," Janice said. "It was a real pleasure seeing you."

"Good-bye." The children nodded, and she offered her right cheek to him. He kissed it lingeringly. She had been just getting over her period, she said. She rarely had an orgasm the first time with a partner, and she never did during her period;

he shouldn't mind about that. She would take her pleasure by helping him have his. This phrase remained with Peter eighteen years thereafter, and he wanted to recite it in the parking lot. Their children were at their elbows, however, and there was confusion at the exit ramp. "I remember you," he said.

"Do call." She smiled and was gone.

"Who was that?" Sam asked.

"An old friend," Peter said. "Did you enjoy yourself?"

"No."

"Not even the Virginia Reel?"

"I couldn't hear. I don't know the directions and everybody was talking."

"I'm sorry."

Magnanimous, Sam said, "It isn't your fault, Daddy."

"No," he said. "Let's go."

His daughter had grown beautiful. He had been prepared for this but not for its sudden coming, the transformation in one summer from pudgy child to clean-limbed grace. It took him by surprise. In the grocery store or post office he watched men watching her—their sidelong glances or open admiration, the space they gave her where she walked or banter at the checkout line. She wore shorts and a halter; her breasts were unbound. The length of her legs and the way that they tapered, the ridge of her pelvis and the hooded stare she offered when he asked her for more coffee—all of this, he told himself, had altered overnight. The telephone rang incessantly. "Ma Bell's best customer," he said. "'Reach out and touch someone.'"

"They all go through it," Judy said.

"Miss Yellow Pages, 1981. The model for the Princess phone."

"We could get her a separate number at home."

"Yes."

Lucinda took up water skiing with the absolute attentiveness she had shown to Bill. She was out on the bay every

morning. She learned to ski backward, and also with one sla-
lom ski. She would criss-cross her wake, leap and glide. He
watched her from the porch. She would emerge from the
water, dripping, shaking her head, her tank suit the color of
flesh. Wind-surfers angled past their house in what he came to
think of as a purposeful display. The sun unrolled a golden
carpet in the waters where she swam. "Our Venus on the half
shell," Peter said.

She also went swimming at night. She said she loved the
freedom of it, chilly black water and phosphor and not knowing when you shut your eyes where you were in the water or
why, not knowing if the thing that bit you was your buddy or a
crab. "Be careful, Lucy," he said. She said she was being careful, and under the influence of the Crab it didn't matter anyway
what bit you in the night. What was really copacetic was celes-
tial navigation. It meant learning how to tell the signs up in the
zodiac, to know the difference, say, between Orion and Sagittarius. She bet he'd never know the difference between Sagittarius and Orion if he was forced to steer by them, if Orion
came right down and slapped him in the face.

"Orion's not likely to do that," he said.

"There's shooting stars."

"They don't exactly slap you in the face."

"They do me. Every night when shooting stars come this
direction, I feel it," said his daughter. "Just like a signal."

"From light years away?"

She nodded.

"Henny Penny thought so too," he said. "And Chicken
Little."

"It's a matter of timing. They might have been right."

The speed of her retort alarmed him. "'Live every day,'"
he said, "'as though that day will be your last. Someday you're
bound to be right.'"

"That's from *Breaker Morant*," Lucinda said. "That's his
line, isn't it?"

"You saw *Breaker Morant?*"

"Last Thursday, remember? At the Community Center."

She was escaping him, he knew, her memories and knowledge no longer his to control. "I worry anyhow," said Peter, "about this nighttime swimming."

"I'll be careful."

"Promise?"

"Yes." She was placatory, dismissive; her horoscope instructed her to go with the flow.

"Can I come too?"

Lucinda turned to him with Judy's tolerance. "It's a free ocean," she said.

His most recent passion was for a photograph. He had been leafing through the autobiography of a movie star. The man was a great and advertised rake; he had squired leading ladies since the thirties and was—or so the flap copy claimed—"baring all." He told about his love affair with a figure skater and what she did with him one afternoon in the practice rink; he told about his walk-on roles in pornographic films. He had worn a fake beard and wig. One underground classic kept the camera focused "between navel and knee"; he said he had been widely recognized nevertheless. He told about the hiring system in Hollywood's heyday and the degree of business acumen in starlets who start on the couch. He had a chapter called "3-D: Drink, Dogs and Drugs." He listed blondes, brunettes and redheads in terms of their competency on horseback and in bed; he had been married six times.

One woman, however, commanded the author's respect. Peter saw her photograph. She had been reading a book. The other women in the photo section were wearing bikinis or low-cut gowns; they were smiling at the camera or brandishing pistols and whips. But Isabella Morris was attending to the text. Her brow was lightly furrowed, her posture upright yet relaxed; she sat in a white deck chair on what seemed to be a porch. Her dress was white; it buttoned to her throat. Peter recognized this woman as a woman he had known.

Her last name when he met her was D'Augremont, not Morris; she had been sixty, and frail. She was the aging mother of a briefly famous singer he had dated in New York. She had called him Mr. Danto with formality that felt unforced; he had been their houseguest in Katonah. She discussed Camus and Gaston Bachelard with him at breakfast, after he had spent the night disporting in her daughter's arms. He needed sleep. He crept back to his quarters at dawn, and at seven she sounded the gong. It rang in the hallway outside. He would wake and wash and shave, anxious to cover the night's fierce tumult, the way Betty raked her fingernails across his back and bruised his neck. He would drag himself to breakfast where Isabella quartered oranges and offered toast with no crust.

The actor mourned Isabella. She had been the one pure lady in his impure life. He said as much. He said she had no public name and did not belong in a rogues' gallery. They met and courted in Manhattan in the Second World War, and he had been the happiest man, the most entirely blessed on leave. They stayed together at the Plaza, and everything was champagne and violets and declarations of fidelity forever and ever; she had been—here he borrowed a phrase from a script—"a pearl among white peas." He had gone to Hollywood after the war. He spent the first three days just waiting for her call, for Isabella to join him and to share his life. She did not call. Her telephone conversation, when he called, was brief. He accepted an invitation to a yachting party, and there he met a pretty girl and they started dating each other. One night at a restaurant she told him she was pregnant, and he woke up the next morning married, with a whiskey hangover and a telegram slipped under his door that read: DARLING I'LL BE OUT TO JOIN YOU NEXT WEDNESDAY STOP ALL BUSINESS FINISHED BACK EAST STOP I HATE THE PHONE STOP ALL MY LOVE FOREVER ISABELLA.

The actor reproduced this telegram in his book. He be-

rated himself for one whole paragraph, saying he had missed
the opportunity of marriage to a splendid woman because he
was impatient. He would never forgive himself ever; he counseled those who read this text or saw that photograph to pause
a moment for love. Her face was lean. Her nose was patrician,
her eyes downcast. She had dark lipstick on and what looked
like a white wave in her short hair. Since the photograph was
black and white, Peter could not tell for certain—but Isabella
appeared pale, almost unwell. She wore a strand of beads, a
bracelet and no ring. The photograph was dated 1943. She was
to marry someone who later died in the Alps. As a young and
wealthy widow she did not lack for suitors but chose to live
alone. She raised her daughters to be intellectual and athletic
and polite. His girlfriend, Betty, had such enthusiastic orgasms
the instant he entered her that Peter felt irrelevant. She sang
torch songs at The Dugout, then folk-rock, then tried scat-sing-
ing. She strained her vocal chords, however, and was told to
rest. She told him that she did not miss the life of a nightclub
singer, not in the slightest, and would rather be in France. He
did not wish to go to France and they separated without ran-
cor. He missed his toast and marmalade and morning conversation more than he missed her at night.

Peter turned to this photograph often. He had known Isabella well, and had known her daughter intimately. He
admired her good works, her charitable enterprise and un-
flagging determination to aid the deaf. She was fluent in sign
language, and her servants all were deaf. They would clear the
table and offer wine mutely, politely, nodding as he thanked
them until Peter nodded back.

Yet her love affair with the actor had the force of revelation. It was common knowledge once, he read, and made the
gossip columns. The actor's ghostwriter might have written for
permission for the photograph and, perhaps, to ask if she had
anything to say. She would have had nothing to say. She had
told him, Peter, nothing. The image of this society lady as a

supple beauty once, not desiccate and severe but nakedly embracing her lover in the Plaza—this image haunted him. It was a reproach. It argued lost youth, transience, the irretrievable past.

One night he did decide to join Lucinda for a swim. There was a bright three-quarter moon; he looked down from the dune's height at two heads bobbing in the waves. He heard what he could have have sworn was laughter; the heads appeared then disappeared together. He shouted from the stairwell's crest, "Lucy, are you all right?" When he started down, however, he had to watch his footing; his ankle hindered him. The stairs were steep. For a moment he lost sight of her among the waves and rocks. By the time he reached the cliff's base she was standing at the waterline, wrapped in a white towel and holding a dry suit. "I could have sworn you were in trouble," Peter said.

"No, Daddy."

"Was there someone with you?"

"I was diving."

"I saw two heads. I heard you laughing."

"What makes you say that?"

"I was worried," Peter said.

"Don't be. I can swim."

They ascended. She had not answered his question, he knew, and knew not to ask it again. Next morning, she said, "Sagittarius. Ted's a Sagittarius. That's why we get along."

"Who's Ted?" he asked her at breakfast.

"A friend."

"Does he live here?"

"Not all year round," she said. "He comes from Arizona too."

"You go to school in Arizona, remember? You come from Massachusetts."

"Anyway," she said. She helped herself to beach plum jelly. Peter waited. He could hear her eat her toast.

"Anyway what?"

"Anyway nothing. You asked."

"Does he go swimming with you?"

"Yes."

"On the buddy system?"

She looked around the table, sighing. "Why such a federal case? You're making a federal case out of nothing, you know."

"I myself," he said, "was once a Sagittarius. I used to go swimming with girls."

"Big deal."

Peter finished his juice. "The beginning of wisdom," he said, "is knowing when to quit. I never was a Sagittarius. I never went swimming. I'd like to meet Ted."

"Fine," she said. "I'll invite him over."

"Tonight?"

"You're a Taurus," she said. "People don't go around changing their signs."

"I suppose not."

"The leopard his spots," Judy said. She had been frying eggs.

"Will you buy Bill?" he asked.

"I don't know." Lucinda turned to her mother. "I haven't thought about it much."

"Then don't. Bill's doing fine without you, right?" Judy said. "You shouldn't buy a horse unless you want it worse than anything."

"Passata la commedia," said Peter. "Now it's Ted."

Inger left for a tour of America after the last class. She would not return in the fall. They sat, legs touching, in the last row of the lecture hall; she took the seat by the door. *The Flies* had been a success. Their pictures appeared in the *Crimson* together. The portly bespectacled French professor wiped his

lectern before every session, then used a separate handkerchief for his hands and mouth. His specialty was Baudelaire
and the "voyage motif." He sported a bowtie and unwrinkled
suits. He wore pink shirts, always, and had a moustache.

She wanted Peter to accompany her; they could visit the
Grand Canyon together, she said, and San Francisco. There
were cars and relatives and rooms available everywhere; they
could be each other's traveling companion. This proved im-
possible. He had a summer job, and his parents would not
have approved. Her parents would certainly not have approved, and she was planning to visit friends of her parents in
Chicago and Aspen.

She called him every night of the first week they were
apart. She sent him letters from the Grand Canyon and Taos
and Yellowstone Park. He loved, he wrote, her circumlocu-
tions and her funny, twisted English, and he thought about the
hand that wrote it and the wrist and elbows and arm and
shoulder and everything connected to the shoulder.

By degrees, however, Inger's letters grew less frequent
and her language less ardent. He turned his attention elsewhere, and, the last time she called, he was in bed with a girl
from summer school. "This isn't a good time to talk," he said.
When he called back later she told him she would fly to Sweden from New York, not Boston. He could meet her at the
airport if he wished.

He did wish, and he tried to get to New York but could
not find a car and had been planning to attend the Red Sox
game that night. He pictured himself at the airport with Inger,
wrapping his arms around her and declaring with intensity
that they were star-crossed lovers whose paths would cross
again. The picture faded. He knew he could not persuade her
of his vivid passion; it was unpersuasive.

In the year that followed, Peter heard of Inger often. She
became rumor's subject once more. Rumor had it that she
slept with Ingmar Bergman and bore his child but stayed mar-

ried to an Italian industrialist nevertheless. The industrialist was sterile, and she therefore had his sanction to sleep with men of superior qualities and blood. She worked with refugees in Kenya and Thailand; she renounced her singing career but made pornographic films. She became a surgeon in Brazil.

Peter heard one story he did believe to be true. He encountered the director of *The Flies*. The director had prospered; he was returning from the festival at Cannes. *"Les Mouches,"* he said. "Can you believe it? All those years ago . . ." In Cannes, he said to Peter, he had met that Swede again; they were driven in the same car to the village of Valbonne. Ike and Tina Turner were playing in Valbonne, and celebrants from the festival drove up for the last show. He would have known her anywhere, he claimed; she had the same wild accent and green eyes.

The road from Cannes was narrow, and traffic slow. Someone in the party produced cocaine. When it was passed to Inger, she inhaled deeply and started to laugh. She said she had powdered her nose. She called Cannes the end of the world. The director described this with precision, and the image grew actual to Peter. Her long neck was arched, her body taut; she seemed convulsed with mirth. The limousine negotiated a hairpin turn; Inger fell to the floor. She spread her hands and crossed her legs and extended herself as if on a cross. He could not tell if this was a seizure or pose. She lay there, twisted, grinning, till the car reached Club Valbonne—then gathered herself from the floor and walked off.

She had been crazy, the director said. She had absolutely refused to acknowledge him. She had been so spacy it was like the Hayden Planetarium right there in that car, in her eyes. Whatever she was into, she was into absolutely and he, Peter, should be grateful he'd got out.

He picked his way along the beach. Theirs was a rocky

shore, with much litter and weed and many points where boulders made the going difficult. There were clay cliffs and freshwater streams. He walked for a full hour, heading east. The tide had washed away all traces of previous passage; he saw no footprints but his own. He did see Clorox bottles and beer cans, a torn beach sandal on the dunes, charred stumps and rocks in a circle.

Peter favored his ankle, testing footholds, anxious not to hurt himself so far from help. Sweating, he pulled off his shirt. He tied it to the branch of a fallen scrub oak where he could collect it on the journey back. The cliffs behind him had huckleberry, gorse and beach plum; there was poison ivy in abundance also. At his feet was a tangle of skate cases and mussel and horseshoe-crab shells. He came upon the object of his walk.

Two freshwater streams formed a cove. There were clay cliffs on either side, and a brickworks facing north. He had not been there in years. The place was familiar, however, its slope to the shoreline unaltered. Fog increased. Someone had tied a ladder to the scree-strewn dunes, and he clambered up it gratefully. A single brick chimney remained. There was a waterwheel and a network of pulleys and gears. The iron rail had rusted and the sluice had been clogged and silted in. Wooden archways gave on nothing. The struts had sprung and the structure collapsed. Whole timbers lay at his feet. Initials had been carved in them, and hearts, and telephone numbers.

Yet the kiln he had come to was massive, its height intact. Small seabirds fled his approach. They fluttered past him noisily. He pictured the brickworks at work. He saw men shaping clay, then firing it, then stacking and loading the brick on barges and floating them off with the favoring tide. Peter sat. He closed his eyes. Horses would be grazing where men cleared off timber to burn. The waterwheel powered the bellows. It was hot. It was noontime, possibly, and time for lunch;

a gong would sound three times. Men lay beneath the smoke-
stacks or took their ease on the beach. Some chewed tobacco;
some had cigarettes and pipes. They adjusted their caps. They
talked about old Norton and his skinflint ways, the Mosler safe
he had, the carriage, the daughter too who'd just as soon see
you struck dead as smile, the big-mouthed bass at the head of
the creek, the herring run that week. There would be a chop-
ping contest at the fair next Thursday, and Norton's white
Belgian by himself would pull more weight than Brady's team.
The prize at ringtoss was to get to dunk the fireman; it had
been a good year.

He had few friends. He had been a "ladies' man" and now
was a "family man." He had acquaintances, of course, and men
he could consult in need; he was sociable. But on the shore he
felt himself abandoned, distinguished from the sea-wrack only
by his sentient alertness to the distinction as such. And for
an instant even this faded, even that self-consciousness was
washed into transparency. A buoy clanked out in the channel.
In the nearing distance, he heard horns. The dream of fair
women was with him, his daughter taking pride of place; she
frolicked in the waves. The stream had not yet silted in nor
production on the mainland proved more efficient. The barges
had not grounded or been sunk. He pictured three such chim-
neys while yet the brickworks thrived. Demand for brick was
at its height; there were many who sat watching from the cove.
Some sat slack-jawed, dozing, toying with their food or pipes;
some boasted of their prowess or offered their opinion on the
merits of a dog. Some gloried in their birth, some in their
horse. Hope and fuel seemed inexhaustible, the future that is
now the past still flaring, fiery bright.

She twirled and floated, oblivious. She and all her company swam by as though in thrall. The water was his arms. She
was wearing a snorkel and therefore kept her face submerged;
her hair fanned out around her like thick weed. He loved her
unreservedly. Beauty decomposed. Had she been able or will-

ing to listen, he would have told her so. She whistled in the spume.

Peter is thirty-eight years old and an insurance broker in the Berkshires. He plans to build a windmill as an alternative energy source. Now that their daughter is away at school, and Sam so often busy, his wife considers buying into or establishing a business. She is sure-fingered, with a taste for children's clothes; she is gifted at and interested in puppetry also. They do amateur theatricals and pageants for the holidays at home.

The Dantos are a three-car family. He drives a Saab and a Buick sedan and a yellow Datsun pickup truck; his ankle heals more slowly than he hoped. He is afflicted with nostalgia for imagined opportunity that had not been, when offered, opportune.

Judy does the crossword puzzle. "What's eight letters for traitor?" she asks. "Beginning with *q-u.*"

"Quisling."

"That doesn't mean traitor."

"Close enough."

"I looked it up," she says. "It means collaborationist."

"Fellow traveler," he says.

She fills in the letters with pencil, provisionally. When she is certain of a word, she writes the letters with pen.

"Imagine," Peter says, "getting your name known for that. Imagine Mr. Quisling's children, and his cousins and his aunts."

"What was that Frenchman called? The man who ran Vichy?"

"Pierre Laval," he says. "Or *le Maréchal* Pétain. There are a whole host of quislings. But they all have his name."

She lights a cigarette. Her hands, she says, indicate most clearly that she is no longer young. You cannot counterfeit youth with your hands. "What's twelve letters starting with *c,*" Judy asks, "that means both beginning and end?"

"Commencement."

The long reach before him looks calm. Cliffs and thick spruce entanglements rise on either side; the finger of water he follows seems an extension of flesh. It is slate-gray, however, then black when the moon goes down. He has taken on provisions at the head of the fjord, at a harbor he cannot pronounce. There are herring, flatbread, ice, and akvavit.

Northiam
Hall

Martin Rother went to England on a research trip. Following the journey that the poet Harold Emmett made—though his began where Emmett's ended—Martin reached Sussex in August. Emmett had died there on March 23, seventy-one years earlier; this August marked his birth's centennial. It had not gone unnoticed. Martin was approached by an editor in Boston; they ate lunch. The time was ripe, the editor suggested, for a reappraisal.

He liked the suggestion. A modest little book, he thought, to suit the modest talent and the little span of Emmett's life—a cautionary tale about the way success goes hand in glove with failure. There had been a movie, once, based on the poet's career. From cub reporter to war correspondent to barroom

lover to the tubercular genius scribbling deathbed verse—all
this took ninety minutes from the first frame to the last. There
had been armies, flamenco guitarists, pale women wearing
black. Greyhounds sported at the poet's heels while he walked
to Winchelsea, his brow contracted in thought.

Martin planned the biography he would write. It would
have to be conscious, of course, of the irony in overstatement.
By the very use of cliché, the chapter headings that would
trumpet their own stereotype ("A Wand'ring Minstrel," "Para-
dise Lost"), he could undermine the notion that such passion
was original. Emmett had read in schoolbooks how the bareheaded artist must run out to drink in the rain. Friedrich Hölderlin, his model, had come from a walking tour in Switzerland,
saying only, saying always, *"Apollon hat mich geschlagen."*

"Apollo has struck me"—was this the blight of sunstroke
or searing inspiration; did the phrase signal genius or idiocy?
It had been the epigraph for Emmett's first collection, and it
became a kind of motto for his behavior thereafter. Hölderlin
had died old, mad and happy. He spent his final decades com-
posing children's rhymes. But "Apollo" meant enlightenment;
it made of Emmett's indifference to doctors a romantic re-
pudiation that defied not merely common sense but fate.

"I'd write about him warts-and-all," Martin told the editor.

"Certainly. I expect so."

They were lunching in Mulberry Street, on baked stuffed
shrimp. "I'm not even sure I admire him," said Martin. "It will
take a while before I'm sure of that."

The editor drank. He wiped his lips. *"The Quest for
Corvo,"* he said. "Symons wasn't certain what he thought of
Rolfe. "Have you reread it lately?"

This flattery—"Have you *re*read it?"—was not displeasing
to Martin. There were, he thought, points of comparison.
Though Emmett was no Frederick Rolfe and he himself no
Symons, the notion of a quest for an elusive character had its
appeal. He was between projects. The advance would last a

year—eighteen months if he were careful—and he could apply for further research funds. It had been decades, after all, since Emmett was considered major, and Martin was a recognized expert. He had annotated the poet's war and travel verse. His *Selected Letters* had done well.

The wine was Pouilly Fumé, and the editor proposed they risk a second bottle. "Friday." He signaled the waiter. "The office shuts at four. Every secretary in the place has weekend plans for the Vineyard. We could conduct our business far better on route three in a traffic jam on Friday afternoons. That's where you find the world."

"It might be," Martin admitted, "time to reconsider."

"Let's hope so," said the editor. "*I'm* not going to spend my weekend waiting for a ferry. Let's drink to that."

They raised their glasses and touched rims. Then the editor recited, at accurate length, Emmett's poem on the virtues of good friends and bread and wine. Called "Cumpany," it extolled just such celebrations as these, the breaking of bread— *cum pane*—as a ritual partaking of God's body since well before Christ.

"You've done your homework."

"No. I learned that one in school. And I've known Emmett's verse for more years than I care to remember. That's why we're meeting, of course. It's a labor of love and not profit for us. It's something that *ought* to be done."

That *ought* remained with Martin for the next few weeks. The editor's sense of urgency and the veiled imperative gave him a degree of confidence. Elsewhere, he had lost it. A love affair that promised much delivered little; his apartment needed painting and his car needed a drive shaft. Lightning struck his stove one night, inflicting damage only on the stewpot left to simmer and on the element beneath. Yet it seemed a signal: *Apollon.*

Vaguely, Martin envisioned casting the book in retrospect,

beginning with the deathbed scenes and working back to birth. His own interest had been captured by the overt necrophilia of Emmett's final volume; he assumed the reader too might wish to start with death-in-life. He himself was thirty-nine—ten years older than Emmett when he died—and self-professedly a beginner. He enjoyed, he said, three *c*s: cigars, carpentry and companionable women who would let him leave at night. Of the former he had a supply; of the last, at this moment, none. He spent July in the Maine woods, in a cabin he had built, adding a screened porch and deck. The business of buying lumber and the business of composition came to seem related, as if the structure of his book had to be pre-planned.

One morning he woke with a toothache. He had trouble with his teeth and did not want to trust himself to a stranger. So he made an appointment—on an emergency basis—with his own dentist in Boston. He drove the whole distance in pain. His dentist pulled the tooth. "You made the right decision," he told Martin. "I could have tried to save it, but there's just too large an abscess. It would have bothered you sooner or later. *Bon voyage.*"

Returning, he again felt pain; the novocaine wore off. He promised himself a jam jar filled with bourbon, and no ice; he solaced himself with images of dreamless sleep in the hammock he'd slung between pines. He'd wake to rhythmic rocking; Susanna would be back again and clothed in sunlight only, the lead-rope to the hammock coiled around her waist. Smoke poured out from under the hood. He slowed down; smoke increased. Martin coasted to a stop on the road's shoulder; he was fifty miles from Boston and eighty from his home.

He stepped out and opened the hood. The radiator was a geyser; it spewed forth green water and steam. A truck pulled up behind him and a bearded man in overalls approached. He leaned over, considered the engine, then smiled at Martin mirthlessly. "Cain't fix that with no Silver Seal," he said.

"Thank you for stopping."

"No problem. This is your problem." The mechanic pointed to the radiator. "We'll go up and get us another." He ran a junkyard, it turned out; his name was Thomas Larrabee. He produced a toolbox. "Thirty-five bucks plus the old one," he announced. "That's what it'll cost you. Labor too." Martin nodded. His mouth was aflame. He watched while Thomas Larrabee extracted the old radiator from its casing. They drove together through the back roads of York Corners to a clearing by a quarry where cars huddled, discarded, like the shells of shellfish. There were pyramids of tires. Larrabee stopped in front of the twin to Martin's car. "Ass-end's stove in," he said. "This baby's off its frame. Except the front end ain't been touched. Wait here."

Guard dogs circled. Martin sat. A plastic go-go dancer dangled from the rearview mirror in the truck; her hair was orange and her hip boots purple. Pain clarifies. He made his bed in other beds, his books about the books of other authors. He planned a final feast of steamer clams and lobster and felt ceremonial, aggrieved, at the fact he would eat it alone.

In London he spent several days on Emmett's faded trail. The poet's rooms had been destroyed by a direct hit in the Blitz; those restaurants he patronized were long since closed or changed. His friends had died. This did not trouble Martin; he conceived of Emmett as a solitary. True, the man went to parties and loved riotous assembly and celebrated in his verse the solidarity of men at war. But he moved from place to place displacing, it seemed, nothing. He left no mark on any life but that of his one daughter—whom he marked for life. Had Martin stumbled on a cache of papers or a vivid firsthand recollection, he would have been nonplussed. He told himself his poet loved oblivion; he rented a car and drove south.

The Old Rectory in Northiam had been transformed into a bed-and-breakfast establishment. Martin stayed there, on the upper green behind the church. The first night he went walking and approached the church as bells were rung; he entered silently. Five women hung from ropes. They pulled in sequence, watching one old woman in a shawl who seemed to be the leader and familiar with the beat. If they hesitated pulling, she would count out their numbers: *one* and two and *three* and four *and* five.

Martin's last name, Rother, was the name of the river that divided Kent from Sussex in these parts; his family had once come from the region. He felt no sense of homecoming, however. The closely clipped lawns and the fields of hops and apple orchards had the feel of strangeness, not familiarity. When he said in the Old Rectory that he'd come to study Emmett, they told him that an Emmett lived in town. "Granny Emmett," his landlady said. "And she wouldn't mind your calling, she lives just across the way. With Charley Walters, he's her lodger. In that weatherboard cottage just there." She winked. "Not the way *you're* a lodger, if you take my meaning. He's been living in that house ever since Emmett passed on."

Martin was greeted at the door by the principal bell ringer; she wore the same fringed shawl. She had never heard of Harold Emmett, and her husband's family—"him as is dead" was how she referred to him—came from Manchester. She did not read poetry herself. But as long as he was visiting she'd like to show him through the house, and here was Charley to help. Charley Walters shook his hand. Unwillingly, he entered.

"Look at this," said Granny Emmett. "This used to be the pantry. And he makes a downstairs bathroom, isn't he a clever man?" She turned the bathtaps and water came out; she left them running for a moment, then turned the taps back tightly. "Linoleum," she said. "Until he fixed this flooring it was just cement."

She showed Martin the linen closet and the cupboard's several drawers. She slid out each drawer as if for inspection, then pushed them back flush. "Rollers," Granny Emmett said. "And every single one of them faced with Formica. Such a clever man."

Charley Walters opened doors. He showed where he removed what used to be a closet and how he fixed the kitchen so you'd never notice when you looked it used to be two rooms. Martin admired the white wallpaper and the red-and-blue checked pattern with Beagles playing checkers. "Seven coats of wax," said Granny Emmett. "That's how many coats are on this floor."

She wore a pink housecoat and slippers to match; her shawl had beads on the fringe. She was, she told him proudly, eighty-three. "He's been living here"—she indicated Charley—"since him as is dead passed away. Eleven years." She shook her head. "You'd never know to look at this house the shape it was in when he came."

"It's wonderful," said Martin. "Thank you so much."

"Just a minute," she said. "You mustn't miss upstairs."

"I didn't mean to disturb you."

"This staircase too." She led the way. "Watch your head. This banister. Charley found it down by Hurlbird Close when they were redecorating. So he brings it home in sections and says, 'Bess, we'll have a staircase like the Hurlbirds used to have.'" On the landing, panting, she smiled at Charley fondly. "What a piece of luck."

"Eleven years," said Charley. "We've been busy all the time."

"Look at this closet, for instance," she said. "He made it too. Made everything." She opened the white deal doors. Charley's coats hung like a troupe of bodiless gray privates on parade; a second door disclosed his trousers and shoes. The drawer beneath it held underpants. "Isn't he a tidy man?" she asked.

"Yes."

She reached up and patted his cheek. "It's such a pleasure

to show somebody how much Charley's done for me."

"For *us,*" said Charley.

"He takes pleasure in it too," she said. "He's not above the occasional compliment."

"It's a lovely house you live in."

"We thank you," Granny Emmett said. "For taking so much time out of your busy schedule for a pair of old people like us."

Her words were not ironic. He felt shamed by their sincerity, the mock they made of his own inward mocking and impatience to be free. A plane above them banked, descending for Gatwick. "Nice weather you've had for your visit," said Charley.

"Yes," he said. "It's wonderful. I'll come again. Goodbye."

That June Martin had delivered his high school's commencement address. It had been more than twenty years since Martin had been graduated from the school; he retained few pleasant memories and had not been back. He did not send money or a list of his accomplishments to the *Alumni News;* he attended no reunions. It came as a surprise, therefore, when a letter from the principal invited him to speak; his book on Heinrich Schliemann's Troy had been an inspiration to the eighth-grade class. Their spring-term project was "Hellas," and his biography—here the principal quoted a teacher—had "taught my students more than the *Odyssey* and *Iliad* combined."

Martin composed a speech. He admitted to inadequacy in front of such an audience; only grown-ups were supposed to address the assembly. How had this happened, he asked; how did he make it from the third row to the podium? He claimed the track had been contracted, though it still was a fifth of a mile. He evoked his adolescence, praised his teachers and the love of learning they instilled. He practiced his speech in front of the mirror and the tape recorder, perorating on the word "commencement" as an endlessly valent beginning. He felt a fraud. He remembered, mainly, his chubby, competitive, short-legged self afraid to do a somersault; he remembered his yearnings and boastfulness, his acne, the jostling at lunch. The private school was well situated. It nestled in the hillocks of an expensive suburb; the approach roads had thank-you-ma'ams to cut down on driving speed. He arrived an hour early and walked the campus grounds. No one paid attention; he slung his coat over his shoulder. He qualified, he knew, to be some student's uncle or the only slightly youthful father of a graduating senior. Sauntering toward the tennis court, he felt as self-conscious as ever in his high school days: the wind-blown intellectual, alone.

A pine branch brushed his face. A bush he had not recollected blocked his climbing path. The breeze was warm. He stood where he kissed his first girlfriend, sweat pouring from him after tennis, the Slazenger upright between them like a sword. She pressed against him briefly, saying, "Don't." They were fifteen. She wore a tennis sweater with crossed rackets on her breast. Where had he gone wrong, he asked himself, what turning taken on the way from youth to citizen that left him in this thicket unaccompanied? He moved among the shapes of other people's memories and made them shapely, literate. He would revise his speech.

Martin buttoned his cuffs. He adjusted his tie. He would say how it seemed natural to Schliemann once to scrutinize the sand and locate Troy. There Helen lay with Paris while Hector paced the town walls; this is the rock where great Achilles grieved. You have to look closely enough. You have to adhere to the text. He would ask his ancient instructors to explain it if they could: how have I come to this pass?

The next house he visited was a bungalow named Nautilus. Reginald Hurlbird invited Martin over for Friday at eleven. "It's the second smallest place in town," he said when Martin called. His voice was reedy, high. His family owned Northiam Hall; his uncle had leased it to Emmett. "Just beyond the Esso station," Hurlbird said. "Look to your left at the station, and you'll be at my gate."

The directions were precise, and Martin arrived ten minutes early. An old man wearing a vest and leather gardening gloves was weeding by the holly hedge. He straightened and took off his gloves. "Do come in," said Reginald Hurlbird. "I live alone here now, so please excuse the mess."

There was no mess. The bungalow was trim as a ship's cabin, and the photographs and paintings hung on a level, like portholes. They depicted the sea. A chandelier in the shape of an anchor had two electric candles. Reginald Hurlbird turned on the switch, and the chandelier candles blinked alternately. "Make yourself at home," he said, and indicated a red leather chair. "What are you drinking? A gin and tonic? Wine? Sherry?"

"Thank you."

They sat. They talked about the weather and inflation. Hurlbird remembered having shared a barber with Emmett in 1908. He had been agog, he said, at meeting so famous a figure. Emmett's boots were brown, and shone; he had been extraordinarily polite. That was the sum total of his firsthand recollection, however. "I always say," he said, "that the great man—the *truly* great, I mean—has time for little children. And for animals. I was only a boy, understand. And I've never forgotten how kind he was, how absolutely attentive. People say he was a snob, and I couldn't speak to that. But I *can* speak most emphatically to the way his boots gleamed, and his American accent. . . ."

Reginald Hurlbird had white eyebrows and a white fringe of hair; his clothes sat loosely on his frame, as if he had lost weight. He did not drink. The sherry was acid; Martin consumed it in small sips. He asked about the manor house, and whether he might visit.

"Dear boy, there's nothing to see," Hurlbird said. "I thought you knew."

"Knew what?"

"They never could determine just what caused the blaze. It's such a pity, isn't it, the house stands for five hundred years *without* wiring, and no sooner do they put it in than"—he snapped his fingers—"pop!"

Martin shifted in his seat. He had counted on permission to explore the fabled house. It had figured largely in the poet's work. By all accounts the place had suited him; he liked to take his morning ride on one of two white horses and gallop down the entrance drive to greet arriving guests.

"They plan to fix it up again," said Hurlbird. "I'm dubious. You should see for yourself—quite a job."

"I will." Afflicted by the sense of his intrusiveness, he smiled. He drained his glass.

"That's all I can tell you, I'm afraid. Your poet was—how shall I put it—a bird of passage, wasn't he?" The corner clock chimed the half hour. "He spent so relatively little time in this area. We've been here for six hundred years." He spread his hands. "'From darkness into darkness,'" says Alcuin of York. "One hears so many stories and remembers so very few."

"Were you a sailor?" Martin asked.

"Yes."

"Emmett also loved the sea."

His host's conviviality had been exhausted, however. He stood, an old man in need of his lunch. "I couldn't bring myself to go back to the place. They kept on telling me, 'It's not so bad, Reggie, do visit.' So one day I went and, let me assure you, I turned right round again."

Martin found the manor house. It lay in a valley, at the bottom of a basin the Kent Ditch had shaped. Fog shrouded it, though the surrounding hillside slopes were greenly brilliant. Sheep grazed. He thought he saw a horse. Tall trees he could not name rose from the mist around the roof; there were signs instructing him that this was Private Property, Unauthorized Persons Keep Out.

He entered cautiously. A tractor turned in a far field and then was lost to sight. The drive was graveled, rutted, and it curved. His motion along it seemed stasis; the drive itself appeared to guide the car's four wheels and therefore the fifth in his hands. When he came upon the ruin, he was unprepared.

The garage was intact. It could have contained a fleet of carriages. Martin parked in front of what had been the servants' entrance, possibly; a bathtub blocked the door. There was a disconnected toilet in the anteroom behind, and piles of rubble and brick. A hanging beam triangulated what would have been a passageway; he picked his way forward, came around a standing chimney and found himself in open space that had been Northiam Hall.

There were shards of roofing at his feet. The staircase held. But where the landing should have been there was nothing now: a floorboard like a spear lodged in the earth. Birds scolded him from the black eaves, and something scuttled away in the rubble. He pivoted. The medieval fireplace where the poet roasted lamb and pigs seemed unimpaired. Everywhere beyond was wreckage, the chapel in the northwest tower gone, its stained-glass windows burst. Emmett would have welcomed this, perhaps; Martin cleared himself a place on the lintel. He lit a Schimmelpenninck and he sat.

"Maiden, war is your lover," Emmett had written. "The house watches over/ what you yearningly call cover/ Night, the windhover/ His uncle. What tower/ Like a mote in wind, our/ Own resistance proving power/ In th'assaulting hour/ Might withstand. . . ." He could not remember the rest. Those tortured rhymes, brief stanzas, had been Emmett's hallmark for the time he spent in Northiam; the romantic figure of the virgin on the parapet was transformed in its urgency to a whore awaiting customers. When he moved closer to the sea he would write his lighthouse poems—and the martello-tower series anticipated these. "Bright thrust of lance/ And parrying glance/ The mating dance/ She wants" was the refrain. Martin thought him overrated. The excellence of even his best work was more a matter of bombast than style. And compared to those two poets with whom he was most frequently compared—Hopkins on the one hand, Wilfred Owen on the other—his intricate arrangements of sonority seemed simple. But there was a residue in Emmett, a kind of drained truth waiting at the bottom of his verse like dregs—and to this bitter residue Martin found himself responsive. A phrase like "Home again, the garroting wire, love's stump" was as acidic—or, as Martin had put it earlier, as "subject to accidie"—as Owen at his bleakest or Hopkins when most desolate. His last book was his best. Underneath the posturing—the pomp and silly circumstance—there could be heard the accents of conviction; given time, Martin believed, he might have produced major verse.

Emmett's life, however, was more celebrated than his art. His amorous exploits were legend, as was his fondness for gin. His narrow escape on the slopes of Mont Blanc made headlines all over the world. His heroism under fire, when a correspondent in the Boer War, the *bon mot* with which he greeted those who watched him row across the Golden Horn—these became the touchstones of a minor cult. He was handsome, young, not poor. He left his native Newark without a backward glance; only three sonnets evoke the New Jersey of his birth. And Emmett traveled widely. At twenty-two he'd been around the world; at twenty-six he settled in this structure; at twenty-nine he was dead. For those final years he cultivated the role of the *poète maudit,* half in love with easeful death; friends who told him to consult a doctor were told in no uncertain terms to leave their friend alone. Those who counseled rest cures elsewhere were told the poet knows no rest: "I had rather sleep in Bedlam's bed/ Than chew this hospice bread."

So when he died of tuberculosis there were many who had warned him—many who had held a blood-stained handkerchief while he was wracked and coughing. "Northiam Hall" became a posthumous success. Martin knew the poem well and therefore knew the space he sat in as the banquet hall; he could half persuade himself that Emmett sat beyond the lintel, drinking, dropping scraps from the table for dogs. The dogs were called Alfred and Chips. He held a silver tankard with a glass bottom; he could see his adversary once he drained the glass. The poet raised and emptied it, and his eye was veined with foam; his hand held steady, however, and he did not blink.

Martin lit a second cigar. A photograph of Emmett taken days before he died showed what a friend at bedside called that "level, inward gaze." His black moustache obscured his upper lip. He lay against a pillow, staring straight at the camera lens. This seemed the great conundrum of the life; if Martin came to terms with Emmett's curious willingness to lie in a sickbed with no help from doctors, to give up with no struggle what he'd struggled so to gain—if he could understand the ending, then the middle and beginning might come clear. The biographer, he thought, must be the retina, the glass, the lens; he must see what his subject once saw. Pigeons settled on the chimney. Martin focused on a dropping where his **foot** approached a brick; a skeletal mouse lay encased. It would have been digested by an owl.

"'Alcuin was my name./ I was always in love with wisdom./ Say a prayer for me that you mean/ When you read this writing. . . .'"

Emmett too had quoted from Alcuin of York. The writer has one privilege, he wrote—that of formulating his own epitaph. Martin asked himself, returning, if those who die senescent in a well-warmed bed know something that the youthful poet imagines only chancely. Granny Emmett's house was lit;

her shadow flitted past the window. He wondered had she told the truth when telling him her husband came from another town. "Looks go. They go. Yours will go as mine did," Alcuin had warned. Music drifted on the green: a tune he knew but could not name. Martin stood a moment, listening; there were stringed instruments. Then he made for the Old Rectory and his evening meal.

They served him in the dining room. He ate alone. Susanna studied modern dance. She would have teased him into playfulness, he knew, or roused him from his lethargy; she would have made him celebrate their bodies' fleet union and skill. Yet this dark space and meager serving appeared his rightful portion. Martin lingered over coffee. He drank a second cup. Blood and flesh and bone compacted intricately everywhere; he tapped the ash from his cigar and marveled at his fingers that, five minutes earlier, had manipulated a knife.

He visited Dennisport next. Emmett's final home, it overlooked the coast. Here his friends had gathered while the poet died. His wife and daughter stayed on, however, and when his wife remarried she left Dennisport in care of her daughter; Julie Emmett lived there all her life. She too was briefly married and had one daughter, Sylvia; Sylvia retained her grandfather's family name. Martin knew the lineage, and that Julie spent her life as her father's votary. She treated the house as a shrine. The ill-kept secret of her lesbian entourage added luster, somehow, to the memory of that rampaging masculine presence snuffed out when she was three. She was as gifted as she was reclusive, and she'd filled the house—according to report—with plaster casts and paintings of her father's face.

Sylvia, the granddaughter, would be fifty-three. She answered his letter politely. If he would care to call on Wednesday afternoon at two, she would be at home. She had read his monograph on her grandfather's "Ballads" and the Introduction to *Selected Letters.* She would be pleased to meet its author and show him Dennisport; she referred to Dennisport as though it were some other someone's home. She looked forward to meeting him soon.

This house was unimpressive. It squatted in a grove of leafless elms. Its outer walls were gray unpainted stucco, its roof slate. There was a central chimney with several chimney vents. The windows had neither curtains nor shutters; a latticework of ivy straggled by the door. He waited in the driveway, then advanced. Emmett had written, "We are happy here/ In this small space./ The place would appear/ To erase place/ Giving instead on queer/ Confinements, the sheer Drop and cliff-face/ of Fear. . . ."

Sylvia Emmett appeared in the doorway. "Mr. Rother?"

"Miss Emmett."

"So good of you to come." She offered a strong hand. She was as tall as he, sharp-visaged, wearing a painter's smock. She had wound a scarf around her forehead and hidden what he guessed was clipped gray hair. Her eyes reminded him of Emmett's own: protuberant, large-pupiled, dark.

"Welcome to Dennisport." She moved aside to let him enter.

"Thank you. How long have you lived here?" he asked.

"Oh, all through my childhood. Then lately, when Julie required it." She made a vague, dismissive gesture. "And I've not been much good, I'm afraid, at keeping things trim."

The entrance hallway stank of cats. It was damp and dark, with photographs of Emmett on the near wall and an umbrella stand that held what Sylvia told him were the poet's walking sticks. "That hat too." She pointed. "It's what he wore when it rained. Though mostly he went bareheaded, Julie used to say. Used to say it was the death of him."

The ceiling was discolored, the plaster veined with age. Areas of plaster had buckled altogether. In the dining room he made out a mural—clumsily drawn, faded—of a satyr eating grapes and holding what appeared to be a chicken in its fist. The sky contained both zeppelins and bombs.

"Your mother stayed here during the war?"

"They all did."

"All?"

"Violet, Samantha, Alison." She smiled again and spread her hands. "It was one of Julie's rules that we used each other's first names only. She objected to surnames, you see."

"Is that a portrait of her father?"

"The satyr? Yes."

"She painted him repeatedly, I'm told."

"We must remember, mustn't we, that grandfather died when she was three. So none of these likenesses are, how shall I put it? remembered. Not done from life. One of my own earliest memories is how she studied photographs. With a magnifying glass. . . ."

Sylvia managed to appear both candid and rehearsed. This was not the first time she had conjured up such memories, and it would not be the last. He played the part of the polite inquiring stranger, and she the role of guide. She showed him where the poet slept and how her mother kept the curtains drawn thereafter; this was the one room of the house, Sylvia said, with curtains. That way air could enter while the room remained dark. She said her mother recollected sitting in a darkened room, hearing the poet cough out fairy tales to keep her amused. He whispered stanza after stanza of what sounded like a nonsense poem. Emmett was working, she knew; he was always working. He could not have produced so many volumes otherwise in such a short time; he was working when he climbed Mont Blanc or in the oarless rowboat he memorialized in "Spindrift."

His washstand stood untouched. The silver-backed brushes and combs had strands of what she assured him was her grandfather's hair. The mirror lay face downward on the tabletop. "All this may seem a little silly to you," Sylvia said. "But I tell myself I'm honoring my mother's wishes. And her memory." She hesitated. "Devotion. That doesn't seem so silly, does it?"

Martin had no answer. He picked up a book. It was leather-bound, a copy of *Transvaal and Other Purgatories.* "Devotion," Sylvia said again. "That's what this room represents. And why I want to maintain it. Not because of who lived here or how he died, but because my mother desired a father. . . ."

She stood so close to him he smelled the staleness of her breath. Her clothes gave off an odor also: turpentine. "You're a painter?" Martin asked.

"I paint a little. Yes."

"Is your studio here?"

"Not here," she said. "I wouldn't want to paint in this place. Not with Julie over my shoulder. All those witnesses."

She led him through the house. There were storage rooms and bedrooms and bathrooms, each decorated with the same lean face and goggle eyes. The portraits were in oil. They had been executed over a period of time sufficient for the style to change; they varied both in attitude and mood. At times the face was shown as that of a young celebrant, at times with the green pallor of age.

One portrait held his attention. It showed the poet in the likeness of a troubadour, wearing motley and plucking what appeared to be a mandolin. The landscape was obscured by mist, but two trees—a cypress and an olive—grew together in the top right quadrant of the composition. A horse was suggested there also, tethered, grazing. The whole was eclectic, thick-fingered, but something in the wash of light evoked a courtly clarity, a man who saw the comedy in posturing yet nonetheless wore costumes.

So Julie had painted her father's face in many variations. What Martin could not tell and wanted to discover was if *she*

had seen the comedy in things. If not, he thought, these paintings were the markers of a lifelong grief, a girl so blighted by
her early loss that nothing thereafter could be transformed
into gain. She did a series of portraits of Emmett at a cobbler's
bench, with lightning in the window of the doorway at the left.

His sunburst of notoriety had soon enough been eclipsed;
his name was no household's word but her own. Yet she
painted him exclusively; she worked at nothing else. Her imag-
ination had been hobbled as surely as if with a rope.

Sylvia offered him tea. He said, "With pleasure," and she
said, "We could take it in the garden, if you'd like."

The garden was enclosed. There were straggling apple
trees, rose beds and dahlias; mimosa grew through windows
of what was once a potting shed. Beyond, in the hazy distance,
he could make out a gray line of sea. There was a green iron-
work table with a glass top. She conducted him to a chair,
swiped at a bench with the hem of her smock and asked him,
"Sugar, cream?"

"Please."

She poured from a dark green pot. His cup was chipped.
He had an image, suddenly, of the editor in Boston who knew
Emmett's toast to "Cumpany" by heart. The conjunction of this
garden and that restaurant seemed fitting, like paired paren-
theses or an arc that comes full circle.

"You remain"—Sylvia paused—"compelled by my grandfather also."

"Yes." He tasted the tea.

"You suggested in your letter that your visit here was
motivated by something more than curiosity. . . ."

He nodded. There was a small sunken pool, with lilies,
and a bronze frog squatting in its center. We never quite end
where we planned, he thought; the corner post is two degrees
off true.

"An article?"

"A book," he said. "I'd thought of a biography."

"Yes."

"But you're against it, aren't you?"

"Biography." She watched him. "It's all so very long ago."

"One doesn't feel that in this house."

"Perhaps not. No."

"You are against it, aren't you?"

"Yes."

Martin drank. "If you'd permit me," he said, "I'd like to buy a portrait."

"Which?"

"The troubadour in the workroom."

"There was a film," she said. "You know it, surely: Harold Emmett inventing sonnets in the sunset."

"I've seen it," Martin said.

"It bothered Julie very much. The terms of her will were so stringent. She thought it, oh, an invasion of privacy."

"Hers?"

"His too, I imagine. I'm so sorry." She placed her hand on his. Her fingernails were bitten, broken. "The pictures aren't for sale."

They sat for some moments in silence. A cat emerged and made for Sylvia; it rubbed against her legs. She fed it cream from her saucer. The cat was large, long-haired. "What do you call it?" Martin asked.

"Artemis." She stirred the sugar in her cup, added cream and did not drink. "She used to have a brother, but now we're both alone."

That night in the Old Rectory, he tried to see a pattern in the houses he had seen. There was a weatherboard cottage, a bungalow that emulated a ship's cabin, a ruin, a shrine. There was his cabin by the Allagash and his apartment on Fresh Pond—subleased to a lawyer now who would be unwilling to leave. Martin lit a Davidoff cigarillo; he sat in the upholstered chair. His bedroom had a lithograph of Rye as envisioned in medieval times. The harbor beneath the walled port was crowded with vessels; it was market day. There were cows and pigs and women hawking bread. Above, on the last parapet, there was pageantry. A lady with a flowing scarf leaned forward to gaze at her knight.

Emmett was committed to the forms of chivalry, and he used them often. His "Virelay on the Whippet" urged the heraldic mode. "Winchelsea" was populated by ladies whose bright eyes reflected the sails of an incoming fleet. "A proper man," he wrote, "is one who has fathered a son, built a house and completed a book."

Martin raised the window. Outside, a light rain fell. He felt again, in the rented room, how much he was a trespasser. It had not been intentional. He had hoped to be a witness. But he had witnessed nothing pertinent, no scene that seemed to require him. The lamplight from his window illuminated air. Emmett's teaching had been suicide; he was better left alone. We each must learn to die; exampling helps only a little. Of the three accomplishments of manhood, Martin had managed two—and if he had not fathered a child, that was a function less of chastity than prophylaxis.

He heard the bells of Northiam Church. He shut his eyes and saw again how Granny Emmett hung from ropes, jumping in sequence, her slight weight suspended. He would not remain. He would pack and return in the morning. He would tell the editor that Emmett was a bird of passage and had flown from dark to dark. Those warming themselves by the fire had shivered for an instant only. "Christ," they said, "the wind turns ugly." Then they huddled to the hearth again and held out their hands.

ABOUT
MY
TABLE

TO THE MEMORY OF JOHN GARDNER

Death visited him daily. He did what he could to deny it but could not avert his eyes. Headlines blazoned and newscasters announced it: bombs and strangulations and cancer were the news. Arson increased. The alarm in his smoke detectors at home whistled at him shrilly for no apparent reason in the night.

The engines of war were well oiled. Animals were slaughtered, and the slaughter was called business or a by-product of progress or sport. His Golden retriever, deaf in the right ear, failed to notice a Toyota Celica and was crushed. Torture was a commonplace, and terror; the models in the toothpaste ads grinned at him mirthlessly. What he saw behind the rictus was the skull.

Daniel was thirty-eight. He was not by nature medita-
tive and not, his doctor assured him, ill. "You're under the
weather, that's all. Stop pushing. Get more exercise." His doctor, Chester Allen, was a paddle-tennis buff; paddle tennis
helped him mightily, he said.

"All right."

"It's the weather," Chester said again. "It's those revolu-
tions. How long have you been back from—where was it—
Nicaragua?"

"Fifteen months."

As if that were the appropriate answer, Chester nodded
and told him to dress.

The winter had been brutal; pipes froze. For the first
twenty days of the year, the temperature failed to reach zero; it
was thirty below every night. In cold like that, he told himself,
all things must wither and shrivel. The weather bureau reported it as the second coldest January since the start of rec-
ord-keeping; the pattern of upper-air currents had changed.
The frost went six feet deep. The slope of his wife's shoulders
had lost its youthful buoyancy; his breath was stale. Rats scuttled in the basement; he found their corpses in the disused
cistern by the pump. These he fished out with a trout net and,
holding the net at its full extent, walked them to the woods
behind the house.

Adriana, their daughter, turned four years old on Sunday,
March 8. They gave a birthday party. She had friends from day-
care and the neighborhood; nine little girls arrived. She was
passionate for tootsie rolls; therefore Ann had baked a cake in
the shape of a tootsie roll. Two feet long, a roulage with fudge
icing and a red design that followed the tootsie roll pattern,
the cake was a success. He took photographs. Adriana could
scarcely contain herself; she climbed the chair at the head of
the table before they were ready to eat.

He offered Bloody Marys to the mothers. They praised his

special secret ingredient, and he said it was no secret, just horseradish. Sun slanted through the picture window, illuminating everything so that he needed no flash. The woodstove was hot. Adriana said, "You're the best daddy in the world." He felt both charmed and flattered, though he knew the phrase had been designed to please him. Her voice rose; she announced this to her company. "My daddy's the best daddy in the world." The women smiled; their daughters appeared unconcerned. Ann put on a record, and they played "Pass the apple" till the music stopped and whoever held the apple lost. They then played musical chairs.

This was not easy with four-year-olds; Daniel slowed the pace. The girls would clamber to their chairs and sit there for a moment, as if ascent was what mattered, and location. They switched seats reluctantly. Ann had decorated the room with streamers and balloons and a paper cutout, hung from rafters, with Adriana's name. Each letter was a different color, except for the three yellow A's. He smiled at Ann. "You're the best mommy," he said, "in the whole wide world."

"Darling," she said.

He stopped the music. There were three girls standing in the center of the circle, and two empty chairs. Adriana, rapt, was watching her tootsie roll cake. "This isn't working," he said.

"No."

"Let's let them all be winners."

"Fine." Ann clapped her hands to get the girls' attention. She said that everyone would get a prize, that musical chairs was a silly game anyhow—who wanted to be the winner, if winning meant you were the only one left? "Let's get these chairs back to the table," she said. "Let's eat cake."

She lit the candles. They sang, "Happy birthday, Adriana." The fifth candle, Daniel saw, was a trick candle; it could not be blown out. It sat apart from the four candles signifying her age, and when she blew it guttered down, then sprang back into flame again. "That means good luck," he told her. "That's a good-luck sign."

So then Ann sliced the tootsie roll, and he added ice cream and passed around the plates. There was pizza for the adults, and Champagne. Pouring, Daniel realized that there were sixteen women in the room. He took no pleasure in this but instead felt out of place, as if his chosen comrades had left him for a meeting of some consequence. They were making for a battlefield; he alone was left behind. They were wounded; they were playing poker; they were inspecting ships. The mothers laughed and chatted and emptied their glasses and threw back their hair.

"What's the matter?" Ann approached.

"Nothing."

"What is it?"

"These children," he said. "These beautiful, clean children." He indicated where they sat. "I wish that this could last."

"It lasts," she said. "In memory." She touched his arm. "In those photographs you're forgetting to take." She moved off to the table, dispensing Coca-Cola and apple juice and chocolate milk; Adriana wanted all three.

Yet death comes unannounced, he knew, and holds dominion everywhere. The news next day included a memorial to a lyricist Daniel had interviewed once. They played his songs. They said he had been a committed civil libertarian, a spokesman for the underdog who cried out against repression and the power structure. Daniel remembered, mostly, a spry old man in yellow slacks who wrote about the rural poor—coal miners, apple pickers—for Broadway and for Hollywood. He played nine holes of golf every day. He confided to Daniel that he—like everybody of his generation, like anybody who cared about language and wasn't a plain fool—had started out a poet. He'd intended to outlast John Keats. But Keats died in his twenties, a pauper, and he was in his seventies and rich. There's ways and ways, he'd said; I turn out a good limerick from time to time these mornings. I find my satisfaction where I can. They were drinking by the swimming pool; Daniel had stayed for the night. The lyricist's new wife said, "You don't mind," not making it a question, and removed her bikini top. "I wrote one good song anyhow," his host announced. "Back in the McCarthy days. You're too young to remember what it was really like."

"I watched the hearings," Daniel said. "I admired Joseph Welch."

"But it was just a TV show. If you never met McCarthy, if you never knew the man . . ." His voice trailed off. He was watching his wife do a back dive, then a steady Australian crawl. She flipped again at the pool's near end and commenced the backstroke for a length.

"Which song was that?" Daniel asked.

"They cut it from the show. 'Too risky,' my producer told me. 'Too much a matter of taste.'" He sighed; he rubbed his legs. "It doesn't matter, really, it's all about that fascist and what he did to *Robert's Rules*. That's what I called it, '*Robert's Rules*.' You know, the 'point of order' stuff, the 'point of information, Mr. Chairman,' while you ruin a man's life." He sang, in a thin tenor, "'Do you still beat your wife?'"

She was emerging from the pool, dripping, glistening. She returned to the board and did a front half gainer.

"Tell me," Daniel asked, "why you let them cut it out. If it was a political statement, I mean, and if you knew it was good?"

"It wasn't. Who'd fall for that old gag?" The songwriter finished his drink. "Besides, we didn't need it."

"No?"

"McCarthy croaked," he said. "A week before we opened in New York."

The profile wrote itself. He was an amiable person, with the desire to please. His wife was provocative, he sprightly; they made an impressive pair. Daniel presented it that way anyhow, though he had had his doubts. The dapper little millionaire, with his vegetable extracts and exercise machines, seemed more fearful of extinction than he had cared to admit. He died, the radio announcer said, in his home in Beverly Hills; we all will miss his lyrics and the dream of a community he urged us all to share. Children in every town in America sing his songs of hope. The tribute ended with a chorus from his famous "Goodnight, Gus." They played the original cast version: "Goodnight You and Me and Us."

Thursday morning he read of a death that touched him far more deeply. Theodore Hatch died "after a brief illness" in New York. He was survived by his wife, the former Elizabeth Cummings, two sons and four grandchildren. For twenty years he had been editor in chief of the magazine that offered Daniel his first job. A memorial service was to be conducted at the Princeton Club that Saturday; in lieu of flowers, contributions could be made to the Heart Fund.

"Look at this," he said to Ann.

"At what?"

He tore the page across and handed her the article. She looked at Hatch's picture, dated 1968. "Oh, *no* . . ." She bent her head.

"Heart trouble, I imagine. I didn't know he'd been ill."

"You should go to New York for the service."

"Yes. We all could, if you'd like."

They reminisced at breakfast about the editor's brusque integrity. Daniel had been wary of the man. Then one summer Ann and he went for a week to Martha's Vineyard; they found themselves on an adjacent tennis court to Mr. and Mrs. Hatch's. When the younger couple's court time had elapsed, they were invited for mixed doubles. In tennis clothes, Hatch proved less

prepossessing; he had a paunch and knobby knees and trouble
at the net. Daniel's first serve was too strong; he therefore used
his second serve continually. He worried as to whether this
could be construed a compliment or insult, a breach of eti-
quette. Later, they had cocktails.

"I noticed," said the editor, "you've been holding back
a bit."

"No. Why?"

"That serve. You didn't have to slice it every time."

Daniel made no answer. The silence that followed, however, was comfortable, as if the elder man took pleasure in the
junior's prowess—a pleasure laced with pride at his own acumen in hiring and ability to see through what was after all a
gesture of respect. When he and Ann left the Vineyard, Daniel
received instructions as to the best way back, and that autumn
he received his first feature assignment. It was a cover story on
the underground railway to Canada, the draft resisters' network and a clearing house for Vietnam deserters.

When they moved to New Hampshire in 1977, Daniel
made a living as a free-lance journalist. Yet Hatch retained a
shaping hand, a sure assessment of intention. They would
meet for lunch. Daniel listened to tales about Virginia, the first
time Hatch had seen the sea and what that illimitable blue vista
had appeared to promise. It was a promise, Hatch confessed,
undelivered by his stint in the Pacific in the war. He still
looked for gun emplacements on each beach. Those day sailors out of Edgartown got on his nerves; the outboard motors
were worse. Every time he saw some idiot with a gin and tonic
on a stinkpot, Hatch hoped the thing would sink.

He grew increasingly cranky. His sons were in Australia,
doing God knew what. He complained that all this hoopla
about "investigative journalism" was new dogs up to old tricks.
He himself, he said, had been born with a hatred of grand-
standing; he couldn't help it, it was like an extra thumb. Hatch
told Daniel of his disagreements with the publisher, his con-

cern for his wife's health—she had one kidney and one lung. He offered rambling anecdotes about Puerto Ricans and Irishmen and Poles and Jews and Canucks. But at the end of every lunch, Daniel felt as if he—not his companion—had been loose-tongued and too talkative; he felt unburdened, always, as they puffed at their cigars.

"I wish we'd known," said Ann. "We could have visited."

"I'll call Elizabeth," he said. "I'll tell her how sorry we are."

"Yes. I wish he'd wanted company."

"'Of a brief illness,'" Daniel said. "That means it wasn't cancer. Or not a long one anyhow."

"You ought to go," she said. "On Saturday, I mean."

That afternoon the weather changed; the breeze bore the mild hints of spring. The sky was blue; the ground yielded under his feet. The shadows in the valley sported highlights of deep green. It was sugaring weather, and the sugarhouse at the base of the mountain was sending white plumes skyward. Adriana, back from day-care, asked him why did maples bleed.

"A tree's blood is called sap," he said. "It doesn't hurt the tree."

"Blood isn't always red," she told him.

"No?"

"Blue. It's blue inside you till it gets outside. And that's when it turns colors."

"What a lot you learned today."

"I learned it from Mommy," she said. "Mommy says a tree feels better to know it gets put on pancakes."

"Would you like to see them sugaring?"

She nodded.

"When?"

"Tomorrow, Mommy promised. Or the day that you go to New York."

"Let's all go tomorrow," he said.

She turned from him to enter the house, and he had a vision of her mangled, bullet-riddled body after an attack. He shut his eyes. The indiscriminate killing, the chemical spraying, detention camp, assassination—all the menace and brutality he'd reported on elsewhere seemed come to this valley to haunt him. His daughter, his precious four-year-old hostage to fortune, his sweet and trustful witness—Daniel shook his head to clear it. He exhaled and touched his toes. He picked up fallen branches and made a pile of kindling and carried kindling to the door. He carried two-foot lengths of oak and ash from the stacked wood by the parking lot to the breezeway by the mud room. He was hot from his exertions when at last he went inside.

The third death came next day. Robert Entemann and he had met in college, and the friendship had endured. They kept in touch by letter and the phone. Robert worked for public television out of Boston; he had volunteered for Vietnam. Like Daniel and the others of their graduating class, he had been against the war. But Robert came from military stock and was even more opposed to letting poor blacks fight the battles of the generals and congressmen. He served with the marines until Khe Sanh. He was released with shrapnel in his prostate gland, a knife scar on the right side of his neck that missed the windpipe by two inches, and, he said to Daniel, more information than he wanted about how to make things explode. That can of kerosene, for instance, and that garden fertilizer there—Robert clicked his tongue. They'd kept him for five months in Walter Reed. He still had trouble sleeping, and he hated it when helicopters buzzed the beach.

In the fall of 1980, Daniel wrote on the campaign. He visited Marietta, Ohio, where Candidate Reagan was giving a speech. He was booked into the Lafayette Hotel—a brick pile at the confluence of the Ohio and Muskingum rivers. The town had been named, he learned, in honor of Marie Antoinette. Lafayette had landed on the banks of the Muskingum, thereby instituting tourism from France. This was the place the Northwest Territory called its capital, a place to be proud to call home. Daniel was invited to admire the gun rack in the lobby and the authentic relics of the steamboat days. He was shown the high-water mark on the stairwell, from the year of the great flood.

It was Reagan country, Daniel knew; the circumstance and pageantry left no doubt of that. He had heard the speech before and would hear it again in the morning; he decided to take the night off. He walked down Front Street to an establishment named *The Becky Thatcher*. A paddle-wheeler, it rode in the brown water, with a gangway for the customers to cross. *The Becky Thatcher* had been painted blue and gold and white; there were gaslights in the bar.

He sat on a red leather stool. He ordered a J & B, double. Robert entered. "I can't believe it, Dan," he said. They embraced. "It's been too long," they said. Robert said, let's just not leave this tub, let's have our dinner right here. Where are you staying? Daniel asked, and he said, down the road a bit, in that awful motor inn. They laughed; they were registered for the same floor. I need a friend, said Robert, I couldn't take another night with forty thousand cheerleaders. He's going to win, you know.

All through the meal, the shock of having met in this strange place remained. They took a corner table; Robert took the corner seat. They joked that it was neither coincidence nor fate but only the same travel agent. The food was surprisingly good. They talked about their college years and agreed to go together to the next reunion. Robert was tired, he said; he was either on expense account or eating out of cans.

He drew his hand across his eyes; he'd fallen for a married woman once again. She was a real estate broker from Ipswich, and he ought to have his head examined. How was Daniel's family? he asked; he would like to visit sometime soon and see what a real family was like. Ann and Adriana, Daniel, said, were fine, When Adriana had been born, Robert sent two dozen long-stemmed roses to the hospital The note read, "May she have her mother's looks, and her mother's brains."

"You're welcome," Daniel said. "Whenever."

"Thanks."

"I mean it. Deer season. Whenever. If you like to ski . . ."

"There's Harv and Judy," Robert said. "I ought to see them too. Mostly they just come to the big city and watch me at the studio and wish it was a quiz show so they'd get to be contestants."

"And win prizes," Daniel said. Judy, Robert's sister, had married Harvey Williams, the CPA in town. When he and Ann had first arrived, Daniel looked them up. "My crazy kid brother," said Judy. "And his crazy friends."

A tug maneuvered past. It blew its whistle several times. *The Becky Thatcher* rocked.

"I heard a funny thing today. They send more coal and limestone down this river," Robert said, "more tonnage every year than travels the Suez Canal. Or possibly the Panama Canal. I can't remember which."

They would not meet again.

Ann and Daniel married on a clear September morning in Vermont. They were married by a justice of the peace, beneath an elm tree at Ann's parents' country house. Then there was a scheduled reception at an inn two miles away. He was twenty-eight, she twenty-six; they both had been giddy with need. He drove her to the party but they detoured down an unpaved lane and parked in a small turning and made love. He kissed her fingers, then the ring. She pulled her wedding dress above her hips and sat on top of him in the front seat, so as not to appear, later, too badly disarrayed. While she rocked above him and the car rocked to their motion, he noticed, he felt, everything: the perfect square of beauty marks on her arching neck, the color of the maples, the scent of pine and of her perfume, and the startled songbirds disrupted into flight. She was heart-stoppingly his darling, and he told her so. She held him when they finished with a calm unyieldingness; she never ever wanted this to end. She rearranged her stockings, he his pants. They were married, they assured each other, in sickness and in health, and they could be a little late to the receiving line.

When they visited her parents the next year, Daniel drove to see the place. It was not there. He tried again, and with the same result. He became superstitious about it; he knew absolutely where they'd turned and how far they had had to go and where the deer had leaped the puddle, skittering away. He remembered how she looked at him when he proposed they park, how he switched off the ignition and the engine's ticktock cooling while his own breath quickened, as did hers. But he could not find the spot. He hunted it repeatedly; there was no exit from the road between the house and inn. In time he came to see this as a compliment to Ann: without her, he was lost.

Tonight, Daniel promised in the morning, he would make a lucky Friday of this Friday the thirteenth; dinner was to be his treat. He wanted to make Ann a romantic and excellent meal. They staved off boredom that way, sometimes, taking turns as chef.

So after the fish store in town received its shipment, he bought oysters and lobster and shrimp. He next went to the health food shop for fresh asparagus. He then went to the Gourmet Shoppe and ranged along its aisles, looking for the bread and cheese and ladyfingers and lemons and cherries he required. It was raining, a chill, solid rain. The wheels on his shopping cart squealed.

His accountant stood by the cereal shelf. "Hey, buddy," Harvey Williams said. "Have you ever eaten this stuff? What's it like?"

He held out a carton of Swiss Familia—Müsli—for inspection. Daniel told him it was excellent with fruit.

"Judy's gone to Boston," Harvey said. "Or yours truly wouldn't be here. I can't tell Post Toasties from Hostess Twinkies now. It's all a rip-off anyway: you pay more for the product with fewer additives."

Daniel agreed. "What's Judy doing in Boston?"

Harvey positioned the Familia in his cart. "I thought you'd heard."

"No. What?"

"I'm sorry." Harvey looked at him. "I just assumed you knew."

"Knew?"

"Robert," Harvey said. "He was blown up by a package Wednesday night."

He straightened.

"Some son of a bitch," Harvey said. "Some absolutely total stranger sends him a *plastique*. He opens it and . . ." The accountant raised his arm, then made a fist. "I hope they catch the bastard. I hope the bastard dies."

He did not trust his voice. "They know it's a stranger?" he asked.

"I've got to run." The accountant consulted his watch. "When Judy gets back, come on over. She'll tell you what she can."

"I'd be grateful," Daniel said.

They wheeled their purchases to the cash register, Harvey first. He paid and left. Then Daniel did the same and sprinted to the car. On the front seat, a lobster had worked loose from its wet bag. It waved its hammer claw at him, but the claw was pegged and threatless and he shoved the lobster back.

Storm clouds masked the sugarhouse; he drove the final mile in snow. A spasm of revulsion seized him at the fork before his home. He had been jailed once, hungry once, and shot at from a distance several times. This did not make him a hero. He had political convictions that were eroding steadily, and a sense of outrage that was mere plaintiveness now. Three people he had known had died within the week. Yet his reactions had been self-regarding, self-obsessed—as if he, Daniel, and not they had been confronted with mortality. He took the whole thing personally, privately, as though he alone in all this land might mourn. He gripped the wheel. Two men had died in the fullness of time, and he thought about the widow of the one, the failure of the other to invite a deathbed talk. A friend who had reported on the increment of violence became an additional victim; Daniel wondered if they'd failed each other, when and how and where.

He thought about the lives they lived, this business of reportage, until they themselves were news. He had written, lately, on a football game in Tennessee where the players soaked the field beforehand so as to make certain it was mud. Then they used a piglet for the ball. He had written on a helium balloon race, a cockfighting syndicate, settlers in the desert who called themselves survivalists and were stockpiling arms. Robert had reported on the danger to the aquifers, the high-school boy from Newton who was blinded by a bear, Atlanta, outmoded radar systems and an outbreak of plague in the hills. A tow truck, downshifting, roared past.

At home, he told Ann what he'd learned. He went into no details since he had none to tell. Adriana was watching TV. Ernie and the Cookie Monster were capering for joy. Someone spoke to them in Spanish, which they were delighted to acquire. Munitions makers thrived. Ann held him, and they stood together in the kitchen. What he saved out for the compost heap would keep a tribe from starving. "Someone called," she said. "From *Esquire*. They wondered if you'd like to do a story on El Salvador. I told them you'd call back."

"I'll call," he said. "But the answer is no."

"It's all around us, isn't it?"

He nodded. He set about preparing the asparagus and shrimp. "I'll go to New York in the morning," he said. "And come home via Boston."

"Yes."

"Let's have a drink." He opened a bottle of wine.

"Please."

Something scurried in the walls. "Your health," he said.

"And yours."

"Should we get another dog?"

"Not yet," she said. "I don't think I could handle it."

Big Bird appeared. He was cajoling a puppet in a garbage can. He danced with the garbage can lid. The roll of photographs he'd taken at Adriana's party had been developed, Ann said. The shots were wonderful. There was one of Adriana with her mouth so stuffed with cake it looked like she'd swallowed the tootsie roll whole. There was one with her cheeks puckered, ready to blow out the candles, that made her look like a chipmunk, adorable.

He looked up to see her crying. "It's awful," Ann said. "It's so awful."

"Not everything."

"It is."

He set himself to comfort her. Death visited him nightly. It comes when it will come. It could be a furnace malfunction, allergic reaction, rabid bat, oncoming drunk in a van in his lane, suicide, undiagnosed leukemia, handgun in a shopping mall, pilot error, stroke, the purposive assault of some unrecognized opponent, earth, air, water, flame.